MY DESPERATE LOVE DIARY

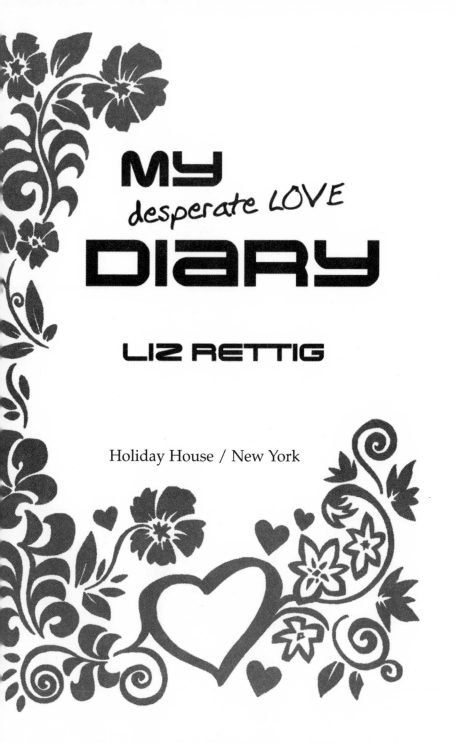

MY
desperate LOVE
DIARY

LIZ RETTIG

Holiday House / New York

Library of Congress Cataloging-in-Publication Data

Rettig, Liz.

[My desperate love diary by Kelly Ann]

My desperate love diary / Liz Rettig. — 1st ed.

p. cm.

First published in Great Britain in 2005 by Corgi Books, under the title: My
desperate love diary by Kelly Ann.

Summary: High-school student Kelly chronicles her year of family problems and
the pursuit of the guy she has a crush on, while not realizing that she herself is the
object of pursuit by Chris, her closest male friend.

ISBN-13: 978-0-8234-2033-9 (hardcover)

[1. Interpersonal relations—Fiction. 2. Family problems—Fiction. 3. Love—Fiction.
4. Diaries—Fiction.] I. Title.

PZ7.R32552My 2007

[Fic]—dc22

2006043647

For my daughter Carol

With special thanks
to Eileen Clarke,
not to mention (though I will)
Guy, Kelly and Annie

Also my long-suffering family

SATURDAY JANUARY 1ST

If I were blonde, the flat chest and spots wouldn't matter so much. Honestly, you could have two heads and if one of them is blonde some bloke will fancy you, but with mouse-brown hair you have to try a lot harder.

It's so depressing. Even my parents have noticed there's something the matter with me. My dad keeps telling me to cheer up, it might never happen. Ha ha. My mum sometimes looks up from her TV long enough to ask what's up with my face.

Have tried to explain how I feel to them. How if they won't let me bleach my hair then the least they could do is pay for breast implants but the response was typical. My dad said not to be so daft, I was fine as I was. My mum just laughed and told me I would know all about it when I was approaching forty and my nipples fell to my knees. That's what happened to her because she'd been a good mother and breast-fed my sister and me and what thanks does she get for it? And she said if she ever met that eejit of a nurse who'd advised her on baby care again she'd tell her where to stick her 'Breast is Best' pamphlet.

But she bought me a Wonderbra and a bottle of Clearasil spot buster for Christmas anyway.

The bra didn't work. As my mum said, no amount of rigging is going to make a cleavage out of two fried eggs. My dad said, 'Why do you always have to call a spade a bloody shovel, Moira? You'll give the girl a complex and she's fine as she is.'

The spots are worse than ever too. My mum says if I were more like my big sister Angela and didn't eat so much chocolate my skin would clear up but my aunt Kate says it's my hormones and my dad says they should all leave me alone and that I'm fine as I am.

It's obvious my family are no help at all. They don't understand what it's like being practically the only girl in the fourth year who hasn't had a boyfriend yet. Only Patricia McPherson is in the same boat as me and she's so ugly even my dad couldn't say she's fine as she is. If she gets a boyfriend before me I'll die of humiliation.

Besides, I'm in love with G. There, I've said it. If you read this, Mum (I know what you're like), it isn't even his real initial so you'll never guess. G is the most gorgeous guy in the whole school and absolutely everyone fancies him like mad. Well, all the females anyway. Well, all the females except Liz and Stephanie who say he's a tosser and so up himself it's not true but they just say that to annoy me. Liz and Stephanie are my best friends but they can be a total pain sometimes.

Anyway, I need to become beautiful so that G will fall madly in love with me and tell everyone I'm his girlfriend and maybe even ask me out. On a date.

Since I'm not blonde or busty I'll just have to concentrate on making every part of my body as perfect as possible so here are my New Year beauty resolutions:

1. To cleanse, tone and moisturize my skin every morning and evening without fail. Even when I'm late for school and I can't find my gym stuff and I have to get a copy of my maths homework from Liz before first period. Absolutely no excuses.

2. To never *ever* squeeze another spot, no matter how much I may want to, even if it is right on the end of my nose or chin.

3. To leave conditioner in for at least three minutes every time I wash my hair and always buy hair products from a proper chemist and never *ever* make my own from 'cheap, natural ingredients you can find in your own kitchen'. If I'm tempted I only have to remember the vinegar rinse that made me smell like a fish and chip shop. Or worse, the shampoo made from Dad's beer that had me grounded for a week and threatened with Al-Ateen.

4. To always have perfectly manicured nails and

never again go to school with chipped varnish. Even when I'm running late, have forgotten my packed lunch, and need to copy my French homework from Stephanie before first period.

5. To eat healthy foods like broccoli and bananas and never again snack on chocolate and crisps when I am bored. Instead I'll write my beauty progress in my diary every single day without fail.

SATURDAY JANUARY 8TH

Mum and Dad went to the pub tonight as usual. My sister's boyfriend Graham came round and gave me a fiver to clear off so I went round to Liz's.

The best thing about Liz is that her room is even more of a pigsty than mine so I can feel really comfortable and smug there.

Liz's dad says he doesn't know why they bothered buying a wardrobe and drawers for her as everything just gets dropped on the floor anyway. He says it's a disgrace but her mum says it's just a phase and she'll grow out of it.

Liz tells them that it's psychologically healthier to be untidy. She asks them if they want her to catch obsessive-compulsive disorder. Her dad says you can't catch obsessive-compulsive disorder, more's the pity, and chance would be a fine thing, their daughter being excessively tidy.

As usual, I had to pick my way carefully into Liz's room looking for the odd bit of carpet not covered with magazines, plates of leftover food, or discarded underwear. It was a bit like trying to cross a wide stream with just a few jutting rocks. Finding a clear space to sit was impossible but Liz swept some of the junk off her bed onto the floor and I settled down next to her.

Offered her a square of chocolate from the huge bar I'd bought on the way there (thanks to Graham's bribe) but she told me she was on a diet. Liz is always on a diet. I don't know why she bothers as, although she's a bit plump, she's blonde and busty but Liz says what really turns guys on is bones with breast, like Victoria Beckham. She says I'm lucky being skinny and if I could just grow breasts guys would be panting after me like dogs outside a butcher's shop.

Then she said she would have a bit of chocolate after all. Just one.

Told Liz about Graham's bribe and that I thought it was gross, my sister having it off with that nerd. My sister could win the Miss No Personality of the Year award and her boyfriend has as much charisma as a boiled potato. Can't imagine them getting excited about anything, especially sex, but they must do it because I've found condoms in her room.

Liz advised me not to look a gift horse in the mouth, referring to the fiver I got as a bribe. She told me there are grosser things than sisters doing it with their boyfriends.

She said her parents still have it away on Sunday mornings.

No, I can't believe it. Liz's mum is so respectable. She buys all her clothes from Marks and Spencer and goes to church every week.

Liz insisted that it was true. She's heard them at it. She said that my parents probably do it too.

I told her that was rubbish; my parents hardly look at each other now. Still, I wonder.

Heard my parents come in tonight and stayed awake to listen carefully. My mum giggled a bit and I heard them pour 'just one more'. Later my mum staggered drunkenly up the stairs. I didn't hear my dad. When I crept down later to check, he was asleep, snoring on the sofa. Thank God for that. Poor Liz.

SUNDAY JANUARY 9TH

School tomorrow – groan – but at least I'll see G again. Must remember to do my hair tonight and blow-dry every hair straight. It's bad enough that I'm not blonde – I have to be cursed with curly hair too.

MONDay JaNUaRy 10TH

Am absolutely over the moon. G actually spoke to me today. This is what happened. I was standing behind him in the dinner queue when all of a sudden he turned round and asked if anyone could lend him fifty pence for lunch as he was a bit short. Luckily, I had the money right there in my hand, and was first to give it to him, and he said, 'Thanks, Kelly Ann.'

He *knows* my name. OK, I know he is in the same class as me for English and maths, but I never thought he actually noticed me.

I only had enough money left for a packet of cheese and onion crisps and a small Coke for lunch but I was so excited I could hardly eat anyway.

Liz says I was a mug to give him money. She says G is a slimy creep who's so up himself it's not true and that anyone can see he's using me but I think Liz is just winding me up. She also said – get this – that I'd be far better off with Chris, as he's much nicer, just as good looking, and fancies me like mad.

Liz is my best friend but she can be incredibly stupid sometimes. Have known Chris since primary school. He's a good mate. We're both interested in football but that's it. The thought of Chris fancying me is totally ludicrous and I'd no more go out with him than I'd snog my own brother, if I had one.

TUESDAY JANUARY 11TH

Am absolutely furious with Chris. He cornered G in the corridor today and demanded that he pay back my fifty pence. G mumbled something about not having anything on him right then. I was *so* embarrassed but I managed to reassure G that it was OK, he could keep the money and not to hesitate if he wanted to borrow any more in the future. It was a tricky situation but I reckon I handled it quite well.

Chris was pretty ashamed of his behaviour, I think, because he turned bright red and walked away.

WEDNESDAY JANUARY 12TH

Have got loads of English homework tonight. Mrs Conner has been awful since her husband left her for his secretary – and yes, you guessed it, the secretary is blonde, of course.

At least all the boring love sonnets have stopped but they've been replaced with all this mad feminist literature about how we're all oppressed by blokes. *As if.* Anyway, tonight we've got a thousand-word essay on 'Are Men Really Necessary Now That the Future Is Female?' Discuss.

G asked if we really had to do this because we've already finished our discursive essay example for our exams. We don't need any more for our folios.

But Mrs Conner said education wasn't just about tests, assessments and examinations. She said she didn't become a teacher to kowtow to examination authorities who don't know their posterior from their mid-arm joint. She said that she hadn't given in to the Tory government by treating her pupils as factory fodder. Nor had she caved in to New Labour by producing robotic pre-programmed Blairites. She said that real education was about nurturing imagination, originality and creativity. That it was her job to foster independent and enquiring minds. She also said that G should stop asking cheeky questions or he would get a punishment exercise and be thrown off the school football team.

G said later that she was a frustrated old bag and probably a dyke and no wonder her husband had left her.

Chris said he was just saying that because Mrs Conner never gave him more than a C-minus for his work.

Used to like Mrs Conner but feel I can no longer respect a teacher who would give a C-minus to someone of G's intelligence and sensitivity.

Anyway, offered to do G's homework for him as he has football practice twice this week. He refused at first – he is so considerate – but I insisted, assuring him that it was no bother at all, and I'd be pleased to do it, and he said, 'OK then, thanks.'

THURSDAY JANUARY 13TH

Stephanie got back from her winter holiday in Tenerife today looking tanned and wonderful. Stephanie is the only daughter of divorced parents and Liz and I are sick as parrots with jealousy.

She has at least four holidays a year – two with each parent – a wardrobe stuffed with designer-label clothes, and fifty pounds per week pocket money. Of course, all this, as she constantly reminds everyone, only partially cushions the trauma of coming from a broken home.

Yeah right, Stephanie! She may be able to fool her parents with that 'innocent victim of divorce' rubbish but we all know she's got it made.

Stephanie's parents are stinking rich so everyone was surprised when she joined our local comprehensive. Her mum said it was because she no longer believed in elitist, divisive education systems but Stephanie says it was because she was expelled from Wotherspoon Halls private boarding school after she was caught having it off with the school gardener's son and called the head-mistress a frustrated old bag. She says she would have got away with it if she hadn't said 'old'.

Stephanie should really be in the fifth year but she was kept back because her boarding school didn't do much in the way of academic stuff. She says all she learned was how to sign her dad's cheques, compose a twelve-course menu and get out of a Porsche without showing her knickers.

Stephanie is the only close friend I have who is definitely not a virgin and we are all very impressed and constantly pump her for information. She once showed us how to put a condom on a cucumber during home economics. Miss McElwee was not happy but Stephanie insisted it was a special type of cling film. Miss McElwee said, who did she think she was kidding, and that she wasn't born yesterday, but Stephanie continued to protest her innocence whilst waving the condomed cucumber about and the whole class was sniggering and tittering so Miss McElwee had to just drop the matter.

I wondered what would happen if my parents got divorced so I asked my mum tonight. She stubbed out her fag and looked at me with a really serious expression. Then she told me that if she and Dad split up there would be the fiercest custody battle the courts had ever seen and wasn't that right, Tom? My dad put down his paper and nodded solemnly in agreement.

I was feeling a bit flattered and excited by the idea. It would be awful for me, of course, torn between loyalty to my mum and my dad but it would be quite romantic in a way too. Maybe my picture would appear in the news-papers with the caption, 'Tragic Teenager in Love Tug Triangle' or some such. Perhaps G would see it and call round to comfort me, pledging his love and support during my ordeal. We would face the glare of publicity together . . . but my mum was talking again and, for once, I listened intently, giving her my full attention.

Oh yes, she continued, there would be no way she would be getting lumbered with me and she expected that my dad would be equally determined. Theirs would be the most titanic struggle in legal history. Then she laughed her stupid screechy laugh and my dad joined in with his horsy guffaws. Very funny. Ha bloody ha.

The only thing worse than my mum and dad arguing and fighting with each other is when they are not arguing and fighting with each other.

FRIDAY JANUARY 14TH

Liz invited me over to watch MTV with her but I told her I couldn't come because I had these two essays to do. Liz said I was mental.

MONDAY JANUARY 17TH

No time to write up my diary at the weekend because of the two essays but it was worth it. When I gave G his copy he said, 'Thanks, Kelly Ann, I owe you one,' and I said it was no bother at all. Any time.

Stephanie said I was stupid and should play harder to get. She said I should 'treat 'em mean and keep 'em keen'.

I just smiled and told her that she didn't understand.

That, sadly, her parent's divorce had caused her to take a jaundiced, cynical view of romance. I explained that true love involved commitment and self-sacrifice and that in any case, G wasn't like other boys. He was different and special.

Stephanie said, 'Bollocks'.

TUESDAY JANUARY 18TH

Liz came round after school and we watched Neighbours. I offered her a chocolate digestive biscuit but she said, no, she was on a diet.

She said she'd done really well today, she'd only had a glass of water with a squirt of lemon juice for breakfast, a packed lunch consisting of one slice of lean chicken, two lettuce leaves and a quarter of a tomato, and fifty grams of grilled fish with a tablespoon of boiled cabbage for dinner. She said that since she'd done so well she would treat herself to a biscuit after all. Just one.

Angela, alias Miss No Personality, later complained that we'd scoffed all the biscuits she'd bought specifically for her and Graham and didn't we see her name written on the tin in large felt-tip letters? She said that she was sick of me taking all her things and she was going to tell Mum and Dad.

I said we had seen her name, but didn't think she'd mind, and that I don't help myself to all her things. For instance, I hadn't used the condoms she kept hidden in her bedroom, even though she hadn't written her name on the package.

She didn't mention the missing biscuits to Mum and Dad after all.

weDNesDay JaNUaRY 19TH

Boring day. G was absent.

THURSDaY JaNUaRY 20TH

miserable day. G still absent. Maybe I should send him a Get Well card?

FRIDaY JaNUaRY 21ST

G back today, briefly, with his mum. Apparently he was caught dogging school and is going to be suspended next week for persistent truanting. So now he is officially banned from coming to school.

Call me daft, but I don't see the point in that. Mrs Conner, our English teacher, says it's an excellent example of irony. I think it's just bloody stupid if you ask me but no one ever does. A whole week without G!

SaTURDaY JaNUaRY 22ND

Utterly mortified today. My mum took me shopping and insisted I get professionally fitted for a bra. We went to this big store where a snooty assistant measured me. I was 32 inches under the bust and 32½ inches over the bust.

She told my mum I wouldn't even fill a pre-trainer A bra and that I'd be better off with a nice warm vest – cheaper too.

Will just have to start saving for implants right away.

SUNDaY JaNUaRY 23RD

Aunt Kate says I might take after my Great-Aunt Winnie and be a late developer. She told me Aunt Winnie was as flat as an ironing board until she got to seventeen when she sprouted breasts the size of pumpkins almost overnight and couldn't walk down any steep hills afterwards for fear of losing her balance and falling over.

But Mum said I might be like her second cousin Maisie, who at forty-six still wears trainer bras and buys her bikinis from the children's department.

Thanks, Mum.

Have got £10.65 left over from Christmas money plus

I get £10 pocket money per week. At this rate I won't be able to save enough money for a boob job until I'm at least twenty-five, by which time I'll be too old to care what I look like.

MONDAY JANUARY 24TH

Boring day. G suspended.

TUESDAY JANUARY 25TH

Robert Burns's birthday.

Mrs Conner says we were supposed to study some of Robert Burns's pieces today because it was his anniversary but in her opinion he was a dissolute, drunken womanizer whose poetry is completely overrated and so instead we would carry on with our analysis of *The Female Eunuch*.

And yes, she knows it isn't part of the prescribed curriculum but she didn't become a teacher to kowtow to exam authorities who don't know their posterior from . . .

WeDNeSDaY JaNUaRY 26TH

Depressing day. Counted twelve spots on my face, one of them right on the tip of my nose.

THURSDaY JaNUaRY 27TH

Miserable day. Fourteen spots now and the one on my nose is getting bigger. Am glad G isn't at school to see me.

FRIDaY JaNUaRY 28TH

Mum asked me what was up and I was stupid enough to tell her.

She said I should be glad that was all I had to worry about. I'd know all about it when I approached forty with a face like a walnut because no one had told me that UV rays caused wrinkles. She said if she ever got her hands on the eejit who sold her the sunbed she would sue him for every penny he had.

But she bought me another bottle of Clearasil spot buster.

SATURDAY JANUARY 29TH

Spots have cleared up a bit. Only ten now and the one on my nose has gone. Happy day.

MONDAY JANUARY 31ST

Hurrah, G back today! Had almost forgotten how gorgeous he is and I think he smiled at me. Well, he smiled in my direction anyway. But even better, during English, G spoke to me and asked if he could have one of my mints. I said yes, of course, and passed him the tube. When he took one and passed it back, I said just to keep the tube.

Unfortunately Mrs Conner later gave him a punishment exercise for eating in class. I tried to defend G by telling her that it was my fault, but she wouldn't relent, instead also giving me a punishment in the form of an essay on the exploitation of women by men throughout the centuries.

But I don't care. The fact remains that G's mouth has touched something that might have been in my mouth if he hadn't first asked me for the mints. Feel that this is a fantastic omen for the future.

Only five spots now.

TUESDAY FEBRUARY 1ST

Am absolutely over the moon. G asked me to do his maths homework for him today as he was busy catching up after his suspension. I think he is beginning to realize how important I am to him and to appreciate my help and devotion.

And, guess what, I have absolutely no spots. Now all I have to do is grow breasts and I will be so beautiful G will instantly fall in love with me.

WEDNESDAY FEBRUARY 2ND

Am so depressed. The spots are back and worse than ever.

Dad says to cheer up it might never happen and Mum asks what's up with my face.

This time, I tell them I have good reason to be

depressed. Didn't they know that Poverty, Injustice and War stalked the globe? That, even as we spoke, there was a famine in Ethiopia and an earthquake in Chile. That political prisoners languished in the jails of ruthless despots and brutal regimes terrorized their own citizens. Weren't they aware that at any moment the entire human race could be annihilated in a nuclear holocaust? How could they be surprised that I was depressed when the world was in the state it was in?

Mum said, 'So the spots are back then.'

THURSDAY FEBRUARY 3RD

My sister Angela – aka Miss No Personality and henceforth referred to in this journal as MNP – is causing trouble for me again.

Liz says that MNP is an anal retentive, which means she is an excessively tidy pain in the you-know-where. She colour co-ordinates her clothes and accessories, irons her bras and knickers and even folds her socks.

Mum and Dad, of course, think the sun shines out of her posterior. She attends a local secretarial college, but to listen to them you'd think she was enrolled at Harvard Business School. They even like her nerdish boyfriend – how sad is that? What self-respecting eighteen-year-old would date for even one more day a guy approved of by parents?

Anyway, MNP's current complaint is that I borrowed a sweater without permission and left make-up stains on the collar.

It's true that I did borrow it but I would have asked her if she had been around at the time. I may have left the faintest smidgen of foundation, about an angstrom thick, on the collar, which anyone but my sister would need a team of forensic scientists to detect, but I would have washed it anyway, some time soon.

Mum was not impressed by my arguments and has grounded me this weekend. I'm sure MNP and Graham are going to be delighted to have my company on Saturday.

FRIDAY FEBRUARY 4TH

MNP has pleaded with Mum to lift my grounding. Mum says that's very forgiving of her, and haven't I got a nice sister, but she is adamant that my punishment should stay.

SATURDAY FEBRUARY 5TH

Parents at pub as usual. Graham gave me a tenner to buzz off to Liz's and keep my mouth shut.

SUNDAY FEBRUARY 6TH

Graham only gave me fifty pence to go to Stephanie's. Obviously he wasn't so interested tonight.

MONDAY FEBRUARY 7TH

Not long until Valentine's day. I suppose I'll be virtually the only girl in the school not to get a card again. It's so unfair. Some people get loads of cards and others, like me, can't even get one.

TUESDAY FEBRUARY 8TH

Mrs Conner has given us another discursive essay today. 'Romantic Love – A Noble Ideal or Just Another Tool for the Oppression of Women?' Discuss.

WEDNESDAY FEBRUARY 9TH

Bought a valentine card for G today. Struggled to write a suitable verse but finally came up with:

Violets are blue,
Daffodils are yellow,

I love you
Please be my fellow.

THURSDAY FEBRUARY 10TH

Made the mistake of asking Liz and Stephanie what they thought of my verse for G during home economics.

Stephanie said it was too tame and suggested:

I love you more with each passing day,
So let's have a quickie unless you're gay.

Liz said that wasn't quite the right tone and scribbled this note which she passed to me:

G, for your body I do hanker,
It's such a pity you're a total—

Miss McElwee caught me with the note and said this wasn't the recipe for pancakes I should be working on. She said she was shocked and disappointed that I could have written such a vulgar and obscene thing. She said she wasn't born yesterday and knew very well what was supposed to rhyme with 'hanker' and it wasn't 'banker' so not to try her patience.

I told her that I had intended to write 'canker', which meant diseased growth and so wasn't very nice but was hardly obscene.

She said to pull the other one and that she was reporting me to Mr Smith, one of the deputy heads.

I told Liz that I was furious with her and there were limits to friendship. She said I could have her new pink nail varnish that I'd liked and I said, don't try to bribe me. So she said I could have her frosted plum eye shadow too, so I said OK then.

FRIDAY FEBRUARY 11TH

Mr Smith said not to give him any baloney about cankers and that he had a good mind to write to my parents and have me suspended. However, he said that there were extenuating circumstances, given that I was talking about G, and that he would let me off this time.

Mrs Conner – who henceforth wants to be called Ms Conner – was very nice to me afterwards. She said she had heard about my referral to Mr Smith for obscene language and considered the complaint sexually biased. She said such language was wrongly considered more acceptable for boys and that she would have spoken up on my behalf if the poem had scanned. As it was, unfortunately, she couldn't defend me on the grounds of literary merit.

I said, 'Thanks, Mrs Conner.'

She said, 'Ms.'

SaTURDaY FeBRUaRY 12TH

Parents went to the pub again. Graham came round but refused to give me anything to go away as he said he knew I was going to see Stephanie anyway. Tight as well as boring. I don't know what MNP sees in him.

Stephanie's bedroom has an en suite bathroom and is stuffed with every imaginable gadget: flat-screen satellite TV and DVD player, computer, state-of-the-art stereo system – you name it, Stephanie's got it. Not that any of this makes up for the loss of a stable, two-parent family life, of course, and actually she envies me. Yeah right.

She was wearing a gorgeous French Connection skirt and top and her hair was professionally streaked with subtle gold highlights. I could tell her a thing or two about envy.

She told me she has a new boyfriend, Ian, who is a pig farm hand. She said she didn't think she'd get a valentine card from him though, as his bicep measurement is bigger than his IQ and he is barely literate. Even if he could write, he wasn't the soppy type.

I asked her what on earth she saw in him. She just gave me a little secret smile and told me I had a lot to learn.

Got back early just to annoy Graham. Maybe he'll be a little more generous next time.

SUNDAY FEBRUARY 13TH

Dreading going to school tomorrow and listening to everyone boasting about their valentine cards.

MONDAY FEBRUARY 14TH
VALENTINE'S DAY

GOT A CARD!!!

It's not signed, of course, but am sure it's from G and he's asked to meet me. It said:

Kelly Ann, please be my girl,
Why not give our love a whirl?
Meet me at the Odeon on Saturday at half past seven
And you will see me in seventh heaven.

Stephanie got around two hundred valentines but, as predicted, none from Ian.

Liz got four valentines, one genuine and the other three in her own handwriting. As Liz says, how can she expect anyone to love her if she doesn't love herself? She also mailed herself a box of Roses chocolates.

Saw G in English today and gave him a secret lovers' kind of smile but he ignored me. Obviously he intends to keep up the pretence until Saturday. What a great sense of humour he has!

TUESDAY FEBRUARY 15TH

Stephanie and Liz are worried that the valentine may not have come from G.

Stephanie asked what if it was from a psychotic killer who'd been secretly stalking me for weeks, and intended to dismember my body, leaving bits of it in black bin bags on rubbish heaps all over town?

Liz said – even worse – it might be from Terry Docherty, the carrot-haired second year with sticky-out ears and buck teeth who pinched my bum in the dinner queue.

It is decided that I will not wait at the Odeon but station myself outside Mario's café diagonally opposite. If G or someone gorgeous turns up, great, but if I see anyone who looks like a mad stalker, or worse, if it's Terry Docherty, I simply go back home unnoticed.

Liz added that in her opinion G is still a slimy creep, but that I have to make my own mistakes, and she hoped things turned out well.

I told Liz that she was being a pompous ass but thanks anyway.

WEDNESDAY FEBRUARY 16TH

Have never snogged anyone and am worried about what to do if G wants to kiss me on Saturday.

27

Practise kissing myself in the full-length mirror in my bedroom.

Sometimes I approach my reflection slowly, with my eyes open, so I can see what I look like close up. Only a few small spots on my forehead. Good.

Other times I close my eyes, put on a sexy expression, and just have to imagine how I look.

The mirror is too smooth and cold so I practise kissing Gerry, the large toy giraffe I've had since I was three.

Of course, my mother chooses this moment to come into my bedroom without knocking and finds me in a passionate clinch with a large stuffed animal. Am utterly mortified but she just gives me a strange look and tells me my dinner is ready.

I hear her go downstairs and say to my dad that she thought it was time I found a boyfriend.

THURSDAY FEBRUARY 17TH

Asked Liz and Stephanie what to do about snogging.

Liz advised that I should keep my mouth closed on the first date – absolutely no tongues – but Stephanie said I should go with my feelings and do what seemed natural.

Liz then said I could allow a bit of breast fondling but on no account let them put their hand up my skirt. She said if they tried to do that, I should guide the hand back to my breasts.

The thought of G trying to fondle my flat chest fills me with horror. I suppose if that happens I will just have to guide his hand up my skirt.

saturday February 19th

6:00 pm
Told my parents I was just going round to Liz's tonight so they can't understand why I'm so nervous and excited.

Have changed outfits three times, and reapplied my make-up six times, on each occasion asking Mum and Dad how I look. My dad always says I look fine but my mum seems worried and puzzled. I heard her tell him, when I was out of the room, that it was time I had a boyfriend but he just said to leave me alone and that I was fine as I was.

Just think, in a few hours I could be out on a date with G. Even better, Monday I'll be able to tell everyone at school G is my boyfriend!

10:00 pm
G didn't turn up. Am devastated.

I kept watch for nearly an hour but no one came. Didn't see anyone I knew at all, except for Chris, who waited ages in the rain for a bus outside the Odeon. I was going to go across and tell him he could have got the number 45 or 17 to his place but didn't want to accidentally bump into my date, or risk my hair frizzing in the wet after spending three hours blow-drying every strand individually.

My first date and I've been stood up. This wouldn't have happened if I were blonde.

SUNDAY FEBRUARY 20TH

My dad says to cheer up, it might never happen. Ha ha. Mum asks what's up with my face. I don't dignify their comments with a reply.

Liz calls and says that G is a slimy creep anyway and at least Terry Docherty didn't turn up.

Stephanie calls and says at least I wasn't hacked to pieces by a crazed lunatic. Nothing helps. My life is over.

Has just occurred to me that maybe G couldn't come because he is seriously ill or perhaps he got knocked down and tragically died on his way to meet me. Feel much better.

MONDAY FEBRUARY 21ST

G is *not dead* and in fact looked perfectly healthy.

TUESDAY FEBRUARY 22ND

Have decided that maybe G got cold feet. Perhaps he doesn't know how much I fancy him and was afraid of rejection. Resolved to make my affection for G clearer.

Liz said I must be joking. She said I couldn't make my feelings more obvious if I went about school with a sandwich board saying on both sides, I FANCY G LIKE MAD.

Stephanie agreed. She said the only other thing I could do to make my intentions clearer was strip off stark naked in front of him and say, 'Let's bonk.'

Liz and Stephanie are my friends but sometimes I despair of them ever understanding someone of G's sensitivity and innate modesty and I tell them so.

Stephanie said, 'Bollocks.'

WEDNESDAY FEBRUARY 23RD

Awful day. Patricia McPherson has got a boyfriend.

OK, it's Terry Docherty, and no girl in her right mind would date such an obnoxious gnome but the horrible fact remains that I am now the only female in the fourth year who has never had a date.

Thank God it's the mid-term holiday and so I will not be subjected to the pitying stares of the entire school.

THURSDAY FEBRUARY 24TH

Stephanie has gone to Paris with her mum and her mum's boyfriend Pierre.

Liz is on a date with yet another boy who has fallen head over heels in love with her cleavage. She moans at me about how difficult it is being a blonde with big boobs – that no one takes her seriously. Yeah right, Liz.

FRIDAY FEBRUARY 25TH

Decided that drastic action was called for, so emptied entire life savings and bought a gel-filled bra. Am now at least an F cup.

Parents collapsed with laughter when they saw me. Dad said I could get done under the Trade Descriptions Act. Hilarious. Mum had a feel of the material and said it reminded her of a waterbed. She also said it stretched credibility even more than it stretched my jumper.

Liz has finished with her boyfriend because he ate nearly all of the Quality Street chocolates he'd brought her as a present so am going round to her place tomorrow night. I'll ask her what she thinks of the bra.

SATURDAY FEBRUARY 26TH

Liz said that personally she thought I was extremely courageous but that I should wear it to school only if I wanted to be a laughing stock. She said that she was my best friend, and that I could count on her loyalty, but that if I insisted on wearing it she would pretend she didn't know me.

I said I got the message.

Liz is on a new diet which involves drinking a slimmer's milkshake for breakfast and lunch then having a sensible balanced meal in the evening. Judging by tonight, a sensible balanced meal includes five slices of pizza, two packets of corn chips, a litre tub of ice-cream, and half a packet of digestive biscuits.

I told her that her diet was about as believable as my cleavage.

SUNDAY FEBRUARY 27TH

Mum was in a foul mood today. All I did was ask her what she wanted for her fortieth birthday next Saturday and she leaped down my throat.

She said what she wanted for her birthday was for people to stop reminding her about it. And she'd thank everyone (here she looked wildly at Dad and MNP too) not to mention again her fast approaching milestone on the way to complete decrepitude.

Furthermore, she said not to give her any of that baloney about 'life beginning at forty' because what really started at forty was prolapsed wombs, thinning hair and dowagers' humps.

Not to mention – though she did – developing droopy eyelids and sagging jowls like a basset hound and a neck like a turkey's wattle. Unless of course she was prepared to hand over half of her and Dad's income to a fabulously wealthy plastic surgeon in order to have a lower face-lift which would make her look as if she was travelling through a wind tunnel. And then of course the other half of their salary would have to be used on an upper half face-lift for the privilege of resembling a permanently surprised Chinese person.

And she was supposed to welcome her official entry to this old crone era? She was expected to actually celebrate her slow slide to the grave? She didn't think so. Then she ran upstairs to her bedroom, banged the door shut and sobbed.

Ha, and people say teenagers are moody!

Can't see why she's so bothered about getting old all of a sudden. After all, she's been old for ages.

Only one more day till I see G.

MONDAY FEBRUARY 28TH

Saw G in English today. He asked to borrow my rubber. Twice! The second time I'm almost sure he smiled at me.

I think it's significant that he chose me but Liz says not. She says he probably asked me because I was the nearest person to him who had a rubber.

Have missed G so much over the holiday break. Wonder if he missed me? Liz says I must be joking.

TUESDAY FEBRUARY 29TH

A leap year. If G had turned up on Valentine's day I could have asked him to marry me.

WEDNESDAY MARCH 1ST

At the back of my home economics jotter, I practised writing my signature substituting G's second name for my own. Got a secret thrill just looking at it. Afterwards, tippexed out the evidence and for security reasons cannot record it here.

THURSDAY MARCH 2ND

Stephanie finally returned from her 'weekend' in Paris. Mr Simmons, our registration and maths teacher, asked her if she and her mother were aware of the official school term and holiday schedule, and if so whether they perceived school as an optional activity, to be fitted in when vacation and other leisure pursuits allowed.

Stephanie replied that, in her view, travel was an important constituent of education and it broadened the mind.

Mr Simmons said that was all very well but that a shopping trip in the Champs-Elysées did nothing to compensate for the revision of simultaneous equations that she'd missed, not to mention the introduction to trigonometry he'd started yesterday. And, by the way, had her mother deigned to write an absence note for her this time or was that too much to ask?

Stephanie said that her mother had been busy lately, but that if he cared to fax her secretary, she was sure something could be arranged.

Mr Simmons said he didn't care to fax anybody's secretary and Stephanie's mum could jolly well write a note like every other parent or they could both take a running jump.

He added that he hadn't become a teacher to be treated like the hired help by stuck-up individuals who wouldn't know a quadratic function if it hit them in the face. That he wasn't prepared to doff his cap, tug his forelock and say 'thank you ma'am and God bless the squire' to anyone. And that furthermore he didn't care whether her mother was Joan of Arc, the Queen of Siam, or the Leader of the Western World. He wanted a note and was that understood?

Stephanie said it was.

FRIDAY MARCH 3RD

Chris asked if I wanted to come and see him play football tomorrow in the school team against St Kentigerns. I like football but almost said no as I was supposed to be meeting Stephanie in Princes Square for a pizza and shopping (I mean pizza and watching Stephanie shop).

Just in time I remembered that G was on the team this year and said that I'd love to, yes please!

Persuaded Liz to go with me. At first she resisted, saying she didn't like football and what was the point of standing around in the rain watching some idiots struggling about in the mud with a stupid ball. However, seeing as I was her friend, and on condition I returned the nail varnish she had 'lent' me, she'd consider it.

SATURDAY MARCH 4TH

My hair frizzed in the drizzle but it was a good game, our team winning three-one.

G looked gorgeous on the pitch and he played fabulously well too. Unfortunately a minor slip resulted in him scoring an own goal and I was shocked to see how unsympathetic his team mates and supporters were. Cries of tosser and worse could be clearly heard around the grounds for some time afterwards. Weren't they aware that even supremely talented players like G sometimes made minor errors of judgement? I thought they were being grossly unfair and told them so but unfortunately my comments were not heard because of the noisy ill-informed jeers and catcalls.

Chris played quite well, scoring two out of the three winning goals. After the match he came up to me and asked what I thought of his performance.

I told him that his first goal had been quite competent although the opposing defence had been extremely lax. His second had, in my opinion, been a lucky fluke and I congratulated him on his amazing good fortune.

I advised him that though in general his shooting and crossing were good, he really needed to work on trapping and tackling.

He looked a bit crestfallen and Liz said afterwards that I should just have said well done but I know that wasn't what Chris would have wanted. Am sure he values my constructive criticism much more than straightforward admiration.

After the match the PE teacher drove most of the team home in the hired minibus but Chris said he would walk back with us girls. G, unfortunately, went on the bus with the others. Chris seemed reluctant to talk any more about football, turning the topic instead to movies.

Liz said she'd just seen *Endless Scream*, which was excellent and was running for one more week at the Odeon. She suggested that Chris and I go see it.

He said that would be a great idea and that he would

pay, seeing as I was saving for my mum's birthday present and he was OK for money this week. What about tomorrow night?

I told him that he wouldn't want to watch a horror movie with me. Although I loved them, I was a total wimp about that kind of stuff, and would probably spend most of the time clutching onto him like a ninny, face buried in his chest, too scared to look at the screen.

But Chris said that he'd put up with it, so I said OK then, we had a 'date'. Ha ha.

SUNDAY MARCH 5TH

Aunt Kate came round with Uncle Jack but Mum just spent the whole time moaning about her approaching birthday. The beginning of the end, she called it, which didn't please Aunt Kate much as she is eight years older than Mum.

Aunt Kate said that things weren't so bad these days and that she'd heard that, when the time came – which was of course a long way off for both off them – HRT could work marvels.

Mum said great, a lifetime of using horse urine products sounded bloody marvellous. Next they'd be suggesting she drink the blood of young virgins to stave off the ageing process.

Uncle Jack said they'd have a job finding young

virgins these days and I thought I saw MNP blush.

Mum told everyone that she didn't want any cards, presents, or cake – nothing on her birthday. She just wanted to ignore the whole thing.

Yeah, right. No one was going to be stupid enough to take her at her word with that one. There would be hell to pay if anything less than a huge fuss with loads of prezzies wasn't ready on the day.

Met Chris outside the Odeon. Linda Robertson was waiting in the queue and she threw me a filthy look. Couldn't figure out why until I remembered that Linda fancies Chris like mad and she probably thought we were going out together.

Pointed this out to Chris and commented on how ridiculous it was. Imagine anyone thinking we were a couple.

'Yeah, imagine,' he said, but he didn't seem to find the idea as hilarious as I did.

The movie was great – what I saw of it. Spent most of the time with my face buried in Chris's chest asking him if it was OK to look now. He must have been totally fed up with me but he didn't complain.

Chris took the same bus as me then walked me home. I said 'See ya' and raced indoors as I still had maths homework to do for G and me.

Can't wait to see him again tomorrow.

MONDAY MARCH 6TH

G said, thanks, he owed me one, and I said that it was no bother, any time.

TUESDAY MARCH 7TH

Am absolutely mortified. There is a stupid rumour going around that Chris and I are an item. I mean, for God's sake, what a totally ridiculous idea! And what if G gets to hear about it? Maybe he will never ask me out.

Chris said that he supposed it was because we were seen at the cinema, it was a perfectly natural assumption to make, and he didn't see what was so ridiculous about it anyway. It wasn't as if he was Quasimodo or anything.

I told him not to be so daft. Of course he was a good-looking bloke and loads of girls fancied him, but c'mon this was him and me they were talking about. It was ludicrous and he had to help me squash the rumours.

He said OK, but then asked, 'just out of curiosity of course', why I didn't fancy him if I thought he was good-looking.

He does ask the most silly questions sometimes. I told him to stop talking rubbish, that he was just Chris, that was all, and I was, well, I was Kelly Ann, and it was perfectly obvious we were just pals.

Chris is great but he can be pretty thick at times.

THURSDAY MARCH 9TH

Bought Mum some perfume – at least now she can smell nice even if she looks old. Mind you, I think she looks not too bad for her age and told her so, but she didn't seem to be too flattered by my observation.

She asked me if I knew the meaning of 'damning with faint praise' and I said that I did. She then asked if I understood the term 'skating on thin ice' and I replied that I'd heard of the metaphor, but couldn't see how it applied here, as I had sincerely meant to compliment her.

Then Dad said something about the First Rule of Holes, which I hadn't heard of, but decided to make myself scarce anyway.

Went round to Liz's. She is currently depressed as she is on a grapefruit and boiled egg only diet and doesn't like either food. She cheered up when she saw I'd brought round some Liquorice Allsorts and decided that she would have 'just one'.

FRIDAY MARCH 10TH

The rumours about me and Chris have died down a little but there's still no sign of G ever asking me out even though he knows for sure I am free.

Stephanie says I've got it all wrong. She says boyfriends are like jobs – easier to find when you've already got one. She told me it would have been better to allow the rumour about me dating Chris to continue, then G would think that at least one other boy found me attractive.

Cornered Chris in the school dinner hall as he was sitting eating his packed lunch and asked him to pretend that we were going out so that G would be jealous and maybe show an interest in me.

Chris went all red and started spluttering. I thought he was choking on his turkey sandwich, and was about to thump him on the back, when he pushed his chair away and spoke.

He said if I were a bloke he would punch me. But then he supposed that if I were a bloke, then I probably wouldn't have made such a bloody insulting suggestion. He said that G was a complete prat and that anyone with half a brain could see what a tosser he was. He told me to go take a hike then stomped off.

I said – to his retreating back – that I would take that as a 'no' then and some friend he was.

Stephanie said that Chris was very sexy when he was angry, and if only he were a little coarser, and a lot less intelligent, she might fancy him herself.

SATURDAY MARCH 11TH

Mum's birthday.

Started quite well with Mum smiling and saying that we shouldn't have, as we all – me, MNP, Aunt Kate and Uncle Jack – presented her with cards and gifts. My dad was working at the garage as usual and so we waited for him to return with the customary wine, flowers and gift before the cake and the for-she's-a-jolly-good-fellow part of the celebrations.

Only he didn't. Well, he did return, but minus the prezzies, so Mum couldn't say he shouldn't have because – well, he hadn't.

We all stared at him with the kind of pitying fascination reserved for a condemned man. You may feel sorry for him but you're glad it isn't you and you don't want to be tainted by association.

Dad looked round wildly for support and blustered something about how she'd said she didn't want anything, and we'd all heard her, hadn't we, but everyone avoided his eyes. Uncle Jack briefly looked as though he might have waded in with a bit of support but a single glance from Aunt Kate stopped him dead.

Mum said nothing. It was really scary. If there is anything more terrifying than Mum ranting and raving when she's mad, it's when she doesn't rant and rave when she's mad.

Anyway, the atmosphere in the house was awful from

then on. Mum even chucked her cake in the bin before slowly, with exaggerated dignity (only spoiled when she tripped on the last step), going upstairs to the bedroom.

Managed to fish the cake out and salvage the bulk of it so we had it for dinner. Delicious. Can't ever imagine being so upset that I wouldn't want to eat cake.

SUNDAY MARCH 12TH

Mum kept up the silent treatment, using me as go-between.

'Tell your father his lunch is in the kitchen.'

'Ask your mother where she keeps the ketchup.'

'Tell your father to look for it himself.'

'Tell your father his dinner is in the oven.'

'Ask your mother where the oven gloves are.'

'Tell him hanging from my lips shouting Tarzan.'

Can't wait to get back to school and I never thought I'd say that.

MONDAY MARCH 13TH

Ms Conner was banging on about gender inequality and male oppression of women again today. She obviously doesn't know about men like my dad and Uncle Jack, or women like Mum and Aunt Kate for that matter.

Still, I do feel sorry for her. It must be awful getting chucked after knowing someone for years. That's the only good thing about never having a boyfriend – at least no one has dumped me yet.

As far as I can see, as soon as you start going out with someone, there is this awful pressure to make sure that you finish with them first. Liz really fancied Greg Stewart in the fifth year but dropped him after two days because it was rumoured he was going to chuck her for someone else. Turned out he had no intention of doing that, and he was gutted, but by then it was too late. Still, as Liz says, in the dumper-dumpee race, you can't hesitate. I suppose Ms Conner is furious she didn't get in first.

G didn't even glance in my direction today. Maybe he isn't ever going to ask me out. Liz said Hallelujah, I was finally seeing sense. Am so depressed.

Dad is still in the doghouse. He bought Mum a dozen red roses, a jumper from Marks, and a new pair of oven gloves but all she said was, 'Tell your father he's too late.'

TUESDAY MARCH 14TH

G spoke to me today! Ha ha, Liz, you're not as smart as you think. He asked if I could help him with some German homework as he had a lot of football practice this week. Unfortunately I don't do German but, thinking quickly, I told him that yeah, sure, I would find someone who could do it. I said he could just leave it with me.

Liz says I'm mad and that G is using me, but I know what I'm doing. I mean, does she think top professional footballers could do as well if they had to bother about German homework every week? Besides, I'm pleased it's me G comes to when he needs support. One day I'm sure it will bring us together.

WEDNESDAY MARCH 15TH

Dad promised Mum a new three-piece suite, and a weekend away at a five-star hotel, so they have made up at last.

Overheard Dad telling Uncle Jack that he can't wait for Mum to get really old and decrepit-looking, then she might be easier and cheaper to please. Uncle Jack said not to count on it. He said he'd already reached that point with Aunt Kate but she was as awkward as ever.

MNP will be away on Saturday at Graham's granny's ruby wedding celebration and will be staying overnight in Edinburgh so Mum said I should stay with Aunt Kate. Asked to stay with Liz instead and she said OK if it's all right with Liz's mum.

THURSDAY MARCH 16TH

Stephanie said this was a brilliant opportunity to throw a party at my place. All we had to do was pretend to our parents we were staying at each other's houses and get cracking with the arrangements as we hadn't got much time.

I told her I could never betray my parents' trust like that. I said it was not in my nature to lie and deceive and besides I might get caught. Stephanie said she would invite G so I agreed immediately.

FRIDAY MARCH 17TH

Stephanie is going to plunder her mum's wine cellar – apparently their house is awash with the stuff and her mum will never notice a few dozen bottles going missing – but Liz and I had to get the beer.

I tried the supermarket first but the woman at the checkout took one look at my face and told me not to make her laugh – she wouldn't be selling me anything stronger than Ribena.

I suggested to Liz that maybe we should wear more make-up but she had a better idea. Back at her place, Liz put on a tight stretch top with a neckline that plunged to somewhere around her navel. With no bra, she looked pretty spectacular.

Next she extracted a skimpy Lycra skirt and told me to try it on. Liz must have worn it last when she was about eight because the hemline hardly reached my crotch and the fit was so tight you could see the outline of each separate buttock. I felt a bit daft but put up with it in the cause of procuring the beer. I did, however, refuse to wear her mother's suspenders and stockings. Imagine Liz's mum wearing something like those under her prissy cotton frocks. It's disgusting.

We set off for the local off-licence. It was a cold night and I was covered in goose bumps but Liz was pleased that her breasts looked even more spectacular than before.

The guy in the shop never took his eyes off my legs and Liz's chest so his gaze didn't travel up as far as our faces, and we were served with no questions asked.

Mum and Dad had already gone, and MNP was out, so we managed to smuggle the booze home with no further problems. Mission accomplished.

Can't wait for tomorrow when G will actually be in my house!

SATURDAY MARCH 18TH

7:00 pm
Am so excited!!! Everything is ready and we're just

waiting for people to get here. What if no one comes? Stephanie says not to be daft. She says who's going to turn down free booze, food and a house devoid of parents.

Liz came over at around one o'clock and helped me prepare the food. We made an assortment of sandwiches: cheese, tuna and chocolate peanut butter (Liz's personal favourite). Then we placed small bowls of digestive biscuits and custard creams on various tables, counters, and armchairs. Ditto bowls of crisps. We had bought a really wide selection of these, from the usual plain, cheese and onion, and salt and vinegar, to the more exotic barbecued bison and toasted hedgehog type stuff so we reckon that we've catered for every taste.

Stephanie and her boyfriend got here about an hour ago. Ian was driving a manure truck and the aroma still clung to him. He is an enormous bloke, a bit like Frankenstein's monster, with a similar IQ but without the bolts. Still, he made short work of hauling in all the stuff from Stephanie's house and will be very handy for repelling any gatecrashers if necessary.

Stephanie had plundered her mum's kitchen and cellar for supplies of peeled prawns, smoked salmon, and a crate of French wines with fancy-sounding names like Pouilly Fuissé, Châteauneuf-du-Pape, and Chablis Grand Cru. Tried some of the Chablis. It was awful, but I added a dash of Coke and it tasted not too bad.

She'd also brought a little black dress that she said

might suit me. Tried it on and it was gorgeous. The short, slightly flared skirt skimmed my hips and showed off my legs, and the top was cleverly cut and draped to make the most of what little assets I have.

Liz says I have good legs and Stephanie tells me my big eyes and fashion model bone structure are a plus. I'd rather have big boobs and blonde hair but I suppose tonight I do look as good as a flat-chested brunette can possibly expect.

Maybe this will be the night that G finally realizes he's been in love with me all along and begs me to be his girlfriend.

SUNDAY MARCH 19TH

Feel awful but at least I'd stopped being sick by the time Mum and Dad got back. The party turned out to be a disaster – for me anyway.

Started off well. Everyone we'd invited got to the house by around nine o'clock and by ten things had really taken off, with people dancing, drinking and generally having a good laugh, especially Stephanie, who was simulating a pole dance using the standard lamp.

G came up to me and for a wonderful moment I thought he was going to ask me to dance but he just said he wanted something stronger than beer to drink.

Went to the kitchen, where I found Mum's Bacardi. Unfortunately, I'd never paid attention when Mum made herself a drink so wasn't sure how it was done.

In the end I just sloshed the rum into a large tumbler until it was around three-quarters full added an ice cube, a sliver of lemon, and a dash of Coke. I was in the hall carrying the drink back to the living room when I saw G coming out of my sister's bedroom upstairs holding aloft a box of condoms. He spotted me and winked suggestively – he must have thought they were mine.

He came down and nudged me against the wall playfully while wagging the condoms in front of my face. I almost spilled the drink, not so much because of being pushed, but the thrill of physical contact with G for the very first time made my hands shake.

Smiling mischievously he told me that he hadn't realized what a very *sophisticated* girl I was and how impressed he was with my, er, maturity and experience.

There was no way I was going to confess that the condoms weren't mine after that so I gave him what I hoped was a sexy, enigmatic smile and said nothing.

He came close, and I thought he was going to kiss me, but then I remembered I'd just finished eating two packets of cheese and onion crisps and so my breath must have been minging. I quickly thrust his Bacardi and Coke towards him.

However, he said he'd changed his mind and insisted

that I drink it instead. G is so thoughtful and generous.

My first gulp was horrible and brought tears to my eyes but I didn't want G to think that I wasn't used to sophisticated stuff like Bacardi so took another slurp right away. The second swig was better and, in fact, I was beginning to feel pretty good.

We went back into the living room, where G loudly announced to everyone that he had found 'Kelly Ann's party balloons', whereupon he offered round the condoms and suggested interesting prizes for the person able to inflate the largest one.

Soon huge, sausage-shaped balloons were floating gently around the room. Everyone thought it was hilarious, except for Chris, who scowled throughout the entire exercise.

G asked me to dance and I didn't feel overawed or nervous at all. Naturally he wanted to dance with me. For the first time in my life I felt beautiful, witty, irresistible.

A slow track was playing and G was actually holding me, his arms wrapped round my waist. Well, maybe round my bum actually but I can't remember exactly. I was vaguely aware that Chris was looking very pissed off and causing some commotion in the corner of the room. Liz appeared to be trying to pacify him with offers of chocolate biscuits and beer but he was having none of it.

Anyway, I was too happy to care and besides I was having difficulty focusing on anything properly, as my vision was getting blurry. I remember putting this odd effect down to the emotion of the moment.

Then it was happening. G pulled away a little and his gaze moved to my mouth. He was going to kiss me! I closed my eyes and assumed what I hoped would be a pouting, sexy expression just like I'd practised in the mirror. However, that's when the trouble started.

With my eyes shut, I began to feel dizzy and started swaying. Next a horrible wave of nausea rolled up from my stomach to my throat. This was definitely not due to passion!

I opened my eyes but the room was spinning and G appeared to have two heads. Putting one hand over my mouth, I managed to lurch away from him and lunge at the living-room door with my free arm. Once in the hall I staggered wildly to the bathroom, pushed open the door, and crawled to the toilet, where I threw up a black-red mixture of Bacardi and Coke, along with partially digested crisps and tuna sandwich.

I remember being horrified when I heard footsteps behind me. I hadn't locked the door and G was going to witness me in this humiliating state! But I needn't have worried. It was only Chris.

I was sick twice more after that. Chris knelt beside me and held my hair back so that it didn't get any vomit on it.

Afterwards, I felt shaky and just sat on the cool tiled floor with my back resting against the wall while Chris wiped my face with a cold, wet flannel. By this time people were knocking on the door as a queue for the loo had formed outside.

We got some funny looks when we came out but I was past caring. I still felt nauseous, and my head was beginning to ache, so Chris helped me upstairs to my room. After chasing Stephanie and her boyfriend out, I lay down on the bed and must have fallen asleep right away as that was the last thing I remember.

Got up very late today feeling even worse than the previous night. My head throbbed, my mouth felt as though someone had force-fed me ashes, and my eyes hurt when Liz opened the curtains of my bedroom with a sarcastic 'And so the sleeping beauty awakes'.

Everyone had gone except for Liz and Stephanie, who had stayed to help with the clear-up. Liz asked what I was going to do about all the Bacardi I'd drunk, as the bottle was nearly empty and my mum was sure to notice. Panicked at first but then Stephanie simply topped it up with water and advised me to 'wing it'.

Liz and Stephanie left around six. By the time Mum and Dad got back at ten I was feeing a bit better so don't think they suspected anything. However, I got stressed when Mum asked Dad to fix her 'just one more' drink.

Mum complained immediately that it was too weak and I felt myself blush. Dad said he'd made it as usual, then he advised Mum she'd better watch it, as starting to think drinks weren't strong enough was one of the first indications of an alcohol problem.

Thought I'd got away with it but Dad cornered me on the stairs before I went off to bed and told me that if I ever tried Mum's Bacardi again, he'd have my guts for garters.

Have always thought this was a particularly disgusting and outdated metaphor – I mean who wears garters any more? – but decided not to press the point.

MONDAY MARCH 20TH

Word has got round about 'my' condoms at the party. It's also rumoured that Chris and I had sex in the toilet. Must say I'm enjoying my femme fatale reputation, as I'm getting a lot of attention from nearly every boy in the school, but find it hard to credit that anyone would believe the story about Chris and me. Still, I won't bother to correct it, as maybe it will make G jealous. G is absent today. Hope he's not ill.

TUESDAY MARCH 21ST

Awful day. Mum found out about the party! Apparently, some nosy neighbours complained about the noise, plus she bumped into Liz's mum.

She went spare at me, threatening to ground me for life, and throw me out of the house. Didn't feel the time was right to point out the contradictory nature of these sanctions.

WEDNESDAY MARCH 22ND

Chris has told everyone that the condoms weren't mine and that I was just being sick in the toilet. Interest in me promptly evaporated quicker than puddles in the Sahara.

Liz has been grounded too and told to tidy her room, so is deeply depressed, especially about the room. Stephanie's allowance has been cut temporarily from fifty pounds per week to twenty-five so she will have to dip into her (considerable) savings in order to buy the new skirt she wants at the weekend.

G is back but seemed to hardly notice me. My spots are back too. Brilliant!

THURSDAY MARCH 23RD

Mum is still on my case about the party. She seems to think that I am now on the road to a life of crime and debauchery and only her constant nagging can prevent it. Today she was banging on about drugs. Had there been any at the party? And not to bother lying to her because she could always tell.

She searched the whole house for evidence but found nothing. (I was more worried about her coming across my diary but it is securely hidden in a place I'm not even going to write here for security purposes. Mind you, I suppose if someone was reading this, then they would know anyway.)

Then she inspected my irises for signs of drug abuse. I wouldn't have minded so much only she was standing very close and I could smell the Bacardi she'd just finished on her breath and the smoke from her fag was stinging my eyes.

She told me that on no account would she tolerate drugs in her home. That if I insisted on ruining my health with dangerous substances it wouldn't be in her house, no way. That if I tried it – even once – I would be thrown out on the street, or worse, taken into care, where I would most likely consort with other degenerates and wind up in prison, dead of an overdose, or pregnant.

SATURDAY MARCH 25TH

Am supposed to be grounded, but when Mum and Dad went off to the pub, Graham offered me a fiver to shove off for a couple of hours at least and we'd all keep quiet about it.

Couldn't go to Liz's as she's still grounded, and Stephanie had a date with Ian, so was forced to call Chris to see if he was free. Luckily he wasn't doing anything and invited me over to watch the match on TV.

His parents seemed surprised to see me, as they had thought Chris was going out with some pals that evening, but said I was very welcome anyway, and his dad offered to show me a selection of Chris's baby photos before watching the match.

The photos were a laugh. I particularly liked the one of Chris in a sailor suit teetering in his mum's high heels, and the one where he was sitting on a potty with chocolate sauce all over his face. Unfortunately Chris grabbed the album away from his dad after that so didn't get to see any more. A pity. I was looking forward to seeing the one of him pretending to have a white beard by looping a sanitary pad around his ears and over his chin.

Chris's mum said wasn't it time his dad put up that shelf in the bathroom, and no, it wouldn't wait till after the match, she wanted it done right then, so Chris and I watched the match on our own.

Manchester United, Chris's team, were playing. Chris's dad is a Rangers supporter but his mum (whose family is Catholic) supports Celtic so they constantly row about football, especially when an Old Firm match is on. To keep out of it Chris used to support Partick Thistle but got fed up with how rubbish they are and now follows Manchester United. Of course both his parents slag him off for supporting an English team but he says it's better than taking one side against the other. Man U were amazing and won two–nil, scoring both goals in the last five minutes.

Chris walked me home then I said 'See ya' and went inside.

Graham was still there and I must say I felt a bit guilty as I just remembered we used up all the condoms at the party for balloons, so I don't suppose he had a very good evening, but he seemed in an OK mood. Quite smug in fact.

Parents got back around midnight as usual. They had 'just one more' drink, also as usual, then my dad sang 'Satisfaction' while strutting about the floor gyrating his hips in a particularly stupid imitation of Mick Jagger. My mum laughed and clapped like a deranged ageing groupie before launching into her own Tina Turner impersonation.

Neighbours had a nerve complaining about the noise at the party last week. It couldn't have been any worse than this.

SUNDAY MARCH 26TH

Parents snappish due to combined hangover and, for the first time, I can sympathize.

MONDAY MARCH 27TH

Stephanie's boyfriend chucked her at the weekend. He said she's too scrawny. Apparently he is looking to the future when he wants to get his own farm and will need a sturdy wife who would not be afraid of hard work and would 'muck in' with the pigs.

I think Liz is secretly pleased that any bloke would dump a girl for being too slim but she offered Stephanie counselling anyway.

She said that the end of an affair is like bereavement and Stephanie would have to work through all the stages of grief. First, there would be Denial, where Stephanie would simply refuse to believe that the relationship was really over. This would be followed by Anger, where she would rail against her fate and perhaps try to plot revenge. Then she would experience Sadness, when she would cry over photographs of them as a happy couple while playing their favourite music. This was an important but dangerous time, when she would have to be careful not to sink into Depression, and Liz and I might have to volunteer to do shifts on a twenty-four-hour suicide watch. Finally would come Acceptance, when healing would be complete, and Stephanie would be ready to move on, strengthened, although scarred, by her experience.

Stephanie said, 'Bollocks', – she was already dating Charlie, a trainee refuse collector with the council.

TUESDAY MARCH 28TH

Mr Dunn, the new permanent religious education teacher, *started today.* He replaces Mr Jones, who retired last month. None of us liked RE so I suppose we gave old Jones a hard time – especially Scott Mulligan, who took the piss out of him at every lesson. Don't think we will be doing that to Mr Dunn though.

Mr Dunn was dressed entirely in black leather biker's gear, had studs pierced in every visible part of his body, with a chain linking his earring to his lip, and what looked like a Hell's Angels tattoo across his knuckles.

He told us that personally he thought religion was a pile of crap but that teaching it kept him off the dole, and allowed him to finance his hobbies of biking and martial arts. He said that he'd heard that we could be a difficult class – and here he stared hard at Scott Mulligan – but that he didn't anticipate any trouble from us. He assured us that, in the unlikely event of anyone giving him any grief, he would break that person's legs and did we understand?

We said that we did.

Then he talked about ancient Rome and the Coliseum. He went into gory details about how Christians were smeared with blood in order to encourage starving lions to eat them. Afterwards, he showed us part of *Gladiator*. Religious education looks like it will be a lot more interesting with Mr Dunn.

WEDNESDAY MARCH 29TH

Scott Mulligan's dad came up to the school to complain to Mr Smith about his son being threatened by the RE teacher. Mr Dunn was summoned to the office to explain himself.

Mr Dunn told Scott's dad that there must have been some misunderstanding. He suggested that he and Mr Mulligan meet privately, man-to-man, and he was sure things could be clarified. But Mr Mulligan said no, he was satisfied Mr Dunn was doing an excellent job, and that kids needed more discipline these days anyway.

THURSDAY MARCH 30TH

Ms Conner asked Mr Dunn to turn the video down. Mr Dunn's classroom is next to her own room and the noise was disturbing her lesson.

Mr Dunn told her to shove it. He said that he would do what he liked and he didn't appreciate her interference.

Ms Conner apologized for grinding her stiletto into his foot but said that she thought she had spotted a nasty, slimy bug that needed squashing. She repeated her request to turn the volume down and he said that he would see to it right away.

FRIDAY MARCH 31ST

The worst day of my life. G has got a girlfriend. Her name is Melissa Campbell. Don't even bother to ask what colour hair she's got. Wish I were dead.

SATURDAY APRIL 1ST

Mum says she's sick of the sight of my moaning face so my grounding is cancelled. She says it's more of a punishment for her than me having a gloomy teenager slouching round the house with a face like a camel that's just swallowed sherbet but that next time I tried anything like that, I would be thrown out on my ear right away, and if that meant I ended up on the streets trapped in a life of crime, prostitution and drugs then so be it. God knows, she'd tried her best, and what thanks did she get for it?

Then she told me that, by the way, she and Dad had been discussing my pocket money and had decided, now that I was older, to double my weekly allowance. I said that was great and thanks a million but then she laughed and screeched, 'April fool – got ya!'

Hilarious.

Went over to see Liz, whose parents had also given in

over her grounding. Discussed how fed up I was with my mouse-brown hair. Liz said that she thought my hair was very nice. That it was not mouse brown but auburn with lovely coppery highlights.

I told her I didn't want auburn with lovely coppery highlights. What I wanted was blonde with blonde highlights. If I had blonde hair, then I would be dating G instead of that tart Melissa bloody Campbell, and that I hated them all, her and every other blonde.

Liz said, 'Thanks a bunch.'

I told her that of course I didn't mean her. That she had blonde hair but wasn't *a blonde* as such. She looked a bit puzzled but nodded uncertainly anyway. It's true though. Liz is too smart and in-your-face to be considered a real blonde. To qualify as a genuine blonde, a female has to have that annoying combination of simpering idiocy combined with colossal ego.

Why, oh why, has G fallen for such shallowness?

SUNDAY APRIL 2ND

Mum is on yet another economy drive. Apparently she's worried about the expense of her three-piece suite and weekend jaunt so we all have to suffer. There's to be no more chocolate digestive biscuits (they just get eaten), only bland tea biscuits no one wants, and our usual Sunday roast has been replaced with tasteless veggie burgers – 'healthier, kinder and cheaper too'.

There's no sign of her economizing on the Silk Cuts, I notice. I really hate her smoking. It stinks the place out. Have tried in the past leaving leaflets lying around about the anti-social nature of nicotine dependency, and the harmful effects of secondary inhalation, but she just used them to light her fags from the fire when she couldn't find her lighter.

Have also noticed the fortune she spends on skin creams. She has different products for her eyes, her neck and the T-panel (nose, forehead and chin, I think). She uses individual lotions for night, day, summer, winter, special occasions and time of month. Some promise to firm, tone and smooth – a bit like a girdle. Others promise to moisturize, nourish, protect and eliminate wrinkles. None have made the slightest bit of difference, as far as I can see, except for the most expensive lotion, which for ninety pounds a gram made her skin go red and peel.

Was probably not the ideal time to remind her about paying the final instalment on my school trip to Paris this June but it was due tomorrow so didn't have much choice. She said, 'I'll Paris you,' a baffling expression in my opinion, and all too typical of the manner in which my parents misuse the English language, but I decided not to point this out.

Anyway, she coughed up eventually, muttering some-thing about how she and Dad worked their fingers to the bone for us and what thanks did they get?

I said, 'Thanks, Mum.'

Not that I'm interested in the trip any more. Life is meaningless now that G has betrayed me. However, Mrs Valentine, our principal French teacher, will go spare if anyone tries to pull out now and school is miserable enough without her on my case as well.

TUESDAY APRIL 4TH

Bumped into melissa Campbell in the corridor today. She acted all casual and friendly as though nothing had happened. I kept my dignity and chatted to her for a while, making no mention of G and the heartache she was causing me. Think I pulled it off. Wouldn't like her to have the satisfaction of knowing how devastated I was. However, Liz said I looked sick.

Moaned to Chris about it at lunch time today. He said that, in his opinion, Melissa and I just weren't in the same league, looks and personality wise. Chris is a good pal but there are times when I wish he weren't quite so bloody blunt.

Ms Conner was banging on about male tyranny again. I know it must have been awful when her husband left her but why just blame men? What about the blonde he ran off with? Don't blondes oppress all us brunettes? We are discriminated against on a daily basis and treated as second-class citizens just because of the colour of our hair and no one does anything about it. Politicians, civil rights activists, social reformers – we're ignored by them all. Where is our Emmeline Pankhurst or Nelson Mandela? Who will campaign for the rights of brunettes for fair and equal access to fit guys in this blonde-dominated world?

Stephanie says if I can't beat 'em I should join 'em. She told me that Alberto (whose real name is Colin), her mum's hairdresser, is very good. She said he is so popular that some people wait for a year for an appointment, but that her mum can speak for me, and I should be able to see him in a couple of weeks when he gets back from New York. She also said that he is quite pricey – a hundred and fifty pounds for the first session but then only sixty pounds a month for a touch-up. She meant my roots, of course. Alberto is gayer than Elton John.

I said I'd think about it. Not.

WEDNESDAY APRIL 5TH

Wonder if I could murder Melissa and get away with it as a crime of passion. Probably have to wait for the Paris trip. Have heard the French are more understanding about stuff like that.

Liz has offered me anger therapy to control my aggressive feelings towards Melissa. She advised me to use a pillow, or soft toy, as a 'hostility channeller'. I was to punch the 'rival object model simulator', i.e. the pillow or soft toy, whilst simultaneously screaming, 'I hate Melissa.'

Tried it tonight using my giraffe. Was quite enjoying the exercise and was adding my own embellishments by throwing the giraffe on the floor, stamping on it and shouting, 'Die, whore!' when, of course, my mum walked in. She said she'd knocked but I hadn't heard her over the din I was making. She gave me a strange look but just asked me to keep the noise down and left.

Later I heard her tell my dad that 'It's time our Kelly Ann had a hobby.'

THURSDAY APRIL 6TH

Totally gutted today. Saw G and Melissa in the play-ground strolling along with an arm around each other's waist. Felt as though they had torn my heart from my ribs and used it for a session of volleyball.

Drastic action is called for. Decided to follow Stephanie's suggestion (with minor alterations) so bought a bottle of GoBlondeNow at five ninety-nine from Boots and asked Liz to help me at the weekend.

Liz said I would need several counselling sessions before undertaking such a dramatic alteration in my appearance. She cautioned me that changing my looks would not necessarily result in the happiness I craved

and that we needed to explore my underlying psychological motivation.

She went on to itemize cases of people who had bat
ears pinned, or nose jobs done, only to find that they were
still dissatisfied with their life because of unresolved
issues of self esteem.

We needed to examine my past in detail in order to
analyse any unresolved conflicts and uncover suppressed
childhood traumas which might be influencing my
decisions today.

Told Liz to can it. Was she going to help me bleach my
hair on Saturday or not? She said OK.

FRIDAY APRIL 7TH

Feel better now that the decision is made. I know Mum
and Dad will go spare at first, but when they see how
beautiful and happy I am as a blonde, they will admit
they were wrong and congratulate me for my brave and
bold action in the teeth of opposition.

Mr Dunn has the hots for, of all people, Ms Conner. He is
always coming into her class asking to borrow a
dictionary, some pencils, chalk – any excuse at all. She, of
course, treats him with utter contempt, grudgingly lend-
ing him the requested items whilst castigating him for his
lack of organization. He listens meekly to her scathing

lectures, his eyes never leaving her face, then says, 'Thanks very much, Mrs Conner.'

She says, 'Ms.'

What a pathetic idiot he is. Any fool can see he is pining after someone completely unsuitable and he has not got a prayer of succeeding ever. When will he get the message? Some people just never learn.

SATURDAY APRIL 8TH

Liz came over to help with my hair. After Mum and Dad left for the pub, Graham made it plain that we weren't welcome, so Liz tormented him with talk of her excellent sense of hearing. She told him she had ears like a bat, capable of detecting the sound of a single leaf falling in autumn, or the tiny scratching of newly hatched caterpillars in spring. Didn't he hear the din they were creating earlier today? She said that making out the rustling of bed sheets or creaking of springs would be no problem to her at all.

Having made certain that his evening was ruined, we turned our attention to the task in hand. Must admit I felt a bit nervous. Imagine me, a blonde at last!

I got out the GoBlondeNow, which I'd hidden in my underwear drawer. I'd selected the Platinum Ash shade and the model on the box looked stunning! I couldn't wait to look like her. The assistant in the chemist's had tried to persuade me to buy a darker, more neutral blonde tone, closer to my own natural colouring, but there was no way I was going for that. I mean, who wants to be a *dark* blonde for God's sake?

Liz and I opened the box and studied the instruction leaflet inside. Apparently we were supposed to do a strand test, where we first carried out the whole procedure on a cut lock of my hair, then waited until the next day to make sure everything worked OK, but we decided to skip that part as it sounded a bit boring, and anyway I wanted to be a blonde right now. Tonight.

We also decided to leave the bleach on for one hour, instead of twenty minutes, just to make sure it really worked.

And it did! I am now definitely blonde. Very blonde. Sort of white, in fact. Whiter than my school shirt, which is getting old and has gone a bit grey.

Liz said that I looked 'er . . . striking', then left rather hurriedly.

Am not sure what to make of my hair. I suppose it's just a matter of getting used to it. No doubt when guys start swarming round, and I have to swat them off, I'll be glad I did it.

SUNDAY APRIL 9TH

10:00 am
Was a bit startled when I looked in the mirror this

morning as I was still sleepy and had forgotten my blonde transformation. Still not sure it's quite right but I guess, as Liz would say, it's a matter of adjusting to my new image. Wonder what Mum and Dad's reaction will be?

10:00 pm
Parents didn't get up until around twelve o'clock. They were completely hung over and so didn't notice anything at first then Mum asked why I was wearing that stupid turban in the house.

Decided to take it off and confront them with a *fait accompli* so to speak. Didn't know what to expect – whether it would be fury, because I had defied them by dyeing my hair, or gasps of admiration at my beauty. In the event their reaction was totally unexpected. After a brief stunned silence they burst into gales of helpless laughter. My mum was bent double, holding onto the sofa for support and screeching that she was going to wet herself – so charming and dignified. My dad said I was the funniest sight he'd seen since Andy McLaughlin's four-year-old boy used the display WC in the Dream Bathrooms shop window to relieve himself – and it wasn't a number one neither.

All this hilarity was undermining my confidence so I went upstairs to study myself in the mirror again. It was true. I didn't look like the blonde model on the box with her Scandinavian complexion and blue eyes. On me, the chalk-white mane simply gave the overall impression that I'd had a terrible fright. I couldn't go to school like this. I'd be a laughing stock.

Maybe I could dye it back but then I remembered Charlotte Conway, who coloured her hair twice in one week – she was always an indecisive type – and it turned green. She'd been so embarrassed she'd had to leave the neighbourhood and was never heard of again. I would have to get professional help.

Called Stephanie, who came round and immediately phoned Alberto in New York, telling him it was an emergency and he'd have to fly back. At first he said he couldn't possibly cut short his business trip and disappoint his wealthy American clients, but then Stephanie mentioned casually that she'd seen his boyfriend, Jason, in a wine bar with a rather attractive blond guy who looked like (though she couldn't swear to it) the male model for Homme underwear. Alberto said he would be booking a seat right away.

MONDAY APRIL 10TH

Refused to go to school looking like this, despite threats from Mum and Dad to alert the Children's Panel to my truancy. And I wasn't to imagine just because the Panel isn't a proper court that they couldn't do anything to me. They would have me declared out of parental control and handed over to the social work department who would throw me into a home full of delinquents, where all my money and possessions would be stolen, and I would be beaten up on a daily basis.

But I held firm. There was no way I was returning to school until they had given me the one hundred and fifty pounds fee for Alberto's services and my hair was fixed. If that meant getting pregnant at the social services six-week assessment centre like all the other female teenagers referred there (it's a mixed sex residential institution and quite a lot of mixing goes on), then so be it.

TUESDAY APRIL 11TH

Parents gave me half the money. The rest had to be made up from my breast implant fund. Guess I'm always going to be a flat-chested brunette.

Alberto reacted with horror to the fact that I'd bleached my own hair. You'd have thought, to hear him talk, that I'd tried to do a spot of triple bypass surgery on myself. 'My dear, you must never, ever so much as touch a single hair of your own head without engaging the services of a professional artiste like myself. Disaster, my love, sheer disaster, as you see.'

He made a great job of my hair though, returning it to its former auburn with coppery bits – what a relief.

Parents refused to write me an absence note so had to forge my own.

Liz suggested I say that I'd had an emotional upset leading to psychological trauma, which resulted in an acute episode of agoraphobia, whereby any attempt to leave my house produced a severe panic reaction.

Stephanie told me just to put that I'd had a bad case of the runs. She assured me that no one would want to enquire too much into a bout of diarrhoea.

Eventually I settled for trichological disorder as, despite the forgery, I didn't want to be too dishonest.

WEDNESDAY APRIL 12TH

Mr Simmons said what on earth was a trichological disorder? Didn't think he'd accept the truth so I muttered something about it being a female complaint, which wasn't a complete lie after all, and he dropped the subject right away.

Ms Conner was talking about Easter today. Our RE teacher Mr Dunn was now on about the Spanish Inquisition and all their implements of torture, but hadn't even mentioned Easter, despite the fact there was less than two weeks to go.

Ms Conner told us that the Christian Church was essentially a patriarchal, hierarchical institution, which had been an instrument of female oppression for two thousand years. For example, they had hijacked the ancient spring celebration which worshipped female fertility, and made it into a remembrance of a patently male God. They had not, however, quite managed to eradicate that powerful symbol of feminine creativity: the egg.

Liz whispered, 'Thank God for that. Easter would be horribly boring without the chocolate eggs.'

Mohammed Sheikh put up his hand and, when invited to comment, opined that it was terrible the Christian Church treating women that way and he was glad he was a Muslim. This was the only time anyone has ever seen Ms Conner lost for words.

THURSDAY APRIL 13TH

Mr Simmons said he'd consulted a dictionary and things had come to a fine state of affairs when the value of education was rated so low that some female thought it quite OK to be absent from school because she was having a bad hair day. Well, not in his register class she didn't. He told me that he had referred the matter to Mr Smith, and that he hoped I'd be severely dealt with.

Was summoned to Mr Smith's office during maths this afternoon. Was rather surprised to find Ms Conner there but she said that she'd heard about my situation and had come to speak on my behalf. After congratulating me on my extensive vocabulary (she thought 'trichological disorder' was most impressive), she launched into my defence.

She told Mr Smith that I was a victim of male obsession with an unrealistic and idealized view of female beauty. She pointed out that for centuries women's mental and physical health had been sacrificed on the altar of men's perverted pursuit of an unnatural, indeed highly artificial, feminine ideal.

Mr Smith was invited to consider, for example, the iniquitous practice of feet binding in China, not to mention, though she did, the artificial neck elongation of women in certain African tribes and the frequent fainting of Victorian women due to too tight corsetry.

And today, she asserted, things were even worse. Mr Smith was asked to contemplate the worrying rise in incidences of eating disorders, not to mention, though she did, the increase in women resorting to plastic surgery.

Now, she went on to say, the whole sad and sorry situation had culminated in a teenage girl, me, whose self esteem had been so damaged by men's insistence on physical perfection that I could not come to school until my hair conformed to present-day male-dominated society's idea of acceptable.

Yet, she continued, the irony was that instead of the support and counsel I required as a victim of this abusive system, I was to be further punished by representatives of the same discredited regime.

Mr Smith interrupted to say that he hoped Ms Conner was not implying that he personally was responsible for centuries of female oppression or that, more to the point, he was at present treating any section of the school community unfairly, and by the way, didn't she have a class to teach?

Ms Conner assured him that his gender bias was probably quite unconscious, and that yes, she did have a class right now, but the need to fight sexual discrimination or prejudice transcended all other responsibilities, and she was prepared to remain in his office all week if necessary to convince him of the justice of my case.

Mr Smith groaned, said that it would not be necessary for her to stay any longer, then turned to me and told me he was prepared to overlook the incident this time but if I ever forged a parent's letter again he would have my guts for garters.

I left relieved but Ms Conner remained. On my way out I heard her expounding on his interesting expression and analysing the imagery of guts and garters. Out of the corner of my eye I could see Mr Smith with his head in his hands, resigned to defeat and a lengthy lecture on the English language.

FRIDAY APRIL 14TH

Last day of term. Probably won't see G for another two

weeks but this time I'm glad. Now that he is going out with Melissa I can't bear to look at either of them.

All the teachers were banging on about how important it was to start revising now for our Standard Grade exams in May so I suppose I might as well do that. There's nothing else in my life now after all.

SATURDAY APRIL 15TH

Slept in until nearly midday so decided to start my revision tomorrow and went over to Stephanie's with Liz.

Stephanie's older brother, Julian, was due to return home from his posh boarding school in England today. Neither of us had met him before, or even seen a photograph, and Liz and I were curious to find out what he was like, especially whether or not he was fanciable. Not that I could ever care for anyone except G, of course, but perhaps if I started dating some sexy guy G would realize he wanted me after all, dump Melissa, and beg me to forgive him.

Julian turned out to be tall and dark but not really fanciable as he was wearing a pink sarong, lilac sandals, and had a coral necklace strung around a rather prominent Adam's apple.

He sat on Stephanie's bed, his large hairy legs sticking out from under his sarong, and chatted easily to us, in a deep masculine voice, as though he were a normal person.

When he left I wasn't sure what, if anything, to say to

Stephanie about her brother as she seemed to accept his appearance as normal, but Liz commented tactfully that it was good that Julian seemed to be in touch with his feminine side, but wasn't his way of dressing a problem at boarding school? Wouldn't he be expelled?

Stephanie laughed and said, God no, the only reason anyone was expelled from her brother's school was poverty. Cross-dressing was, in fact, the fashion this year in the sixth form, but Julian wasn't really into it. He had borrowed the outfit from a pal to annoy his dad, whom he'd be meeting later tonight.

Apparently their dad wanted Julian to join the business he'd founded ten years ago but Julian wasn't interested and had tried everything to convince his dad he was unsuitable for a management job – the pink sarong being his latest attempt.

Can't say I blame him for not wanting to join. The manufacture and marketing of portable toilets may have made his dad a fortune but what would you say if anyone asked you what you did – 'I'm in toilets?' It doesn't bear thinking about.

SUNDaY APRIL 1 6TH

Only three small spots today, but what does it matter how many spots I have if G never looks at me now that he has Melissa?

Was stupid enough to share this thought with Liz who, instead of sympathizing, prattled on endlessly about whether a spot actually existed at all if no one could see it and how philosophers had been pondering these fundamental questions for thousands of years.

Asked Liz if she was actually talking to me at all since I wasn't paying her a blind bit of attention. But this didn't stop her. Finally enquired whether, if no one could hear her scream when I slapped her, she would really feel any pain. She took the hint.

MONDAY APRIL 17TH

Decided to go to the library to study with Stephanie and Liz, and met them outside. It was half past twelve so Liz suggested we get some lunch first. Went for a burger and chips at McDonald's then Stephanie said she'd seen a nice skirt in Fraser's and would we like to give her our opinion on it?

At Fraser's they were doing free make-overs in the cosmetic department so we all had our faces done. Afterwards there didn't seem much point in going to the library as it was getting late so we went to Stephanie's instead.

Her brother was home, dressed this time in blue jeans and white T-shirt. He is quite nice looking in a dark,

Italian sort of way, although his nose is a shade too big. Apparently his tactics had backfired with his father who was now saying that he was no longer prepared to pay sixteen thousand a year in fees for a so-called education, which had resulted in Julian gaining no qualifications worth talking about, and was turning him into a frigging fairy to boot.

Furthermore, his dad had gone on to say that, since Julian obviously thought himself above working in the family firm, he could damned well find himself some other gainful employment, or his allowance would be docked completely.

Julian had gone to the job centre this morning but unfortunately there were no vacancies for poets as yet and they suggested call centre work instead. Julian said he'd think about it.

TUESDAY APRIL 18TH

Went to the library again today, just Liz and me though, as Stephanie and her mum were off to London for a few days of shopping. This time we actually made it through the door. Chris was there, studying hard. He's dead keen to be a doctor and unless you get at least ninety-eight per cent for everything, even PE, over your entire school career, you have no chance of getting accepted for medicine.

Don't know why they insist on people being so bloody brilliant just to be a doctor. Any time I've gone to our GP, he's told me that I've got a bug, there's a lot of it going around, and sent me off, plus or minus an antibiotic prescription. I mean, how smart do you have to be for that?

Can't imagine why anyone would want to be a doctor. Unless of course you happen to be an ugly guy with no personality whatsoever, but still want to guarantee that loads of nurses will fancy you. This doesn't apply to Chris, who's not that bad looking and a good laugh too, and could probably get a date with a nurse without all that hassle, so I don't know why he's interested.

Liz said that Julian had emailed her asking for a date but she'd told him that he should work out his psychological conflicts with his father before embarking on relationships with girls. She said she'd forward his email to me tonight so I could read it. I wonder when guys will ever work out that their emails, far from being private, usually end up being read and dissected by around five thousand females.

After an hour or so, Chris suggested we all go to the café for a Coke, but Liz said she wanted to study some more. This sudden interest in work was surprising, given that she'd spent most of her time browsing among the library's collection of psychology self-help books. Still, we left her to it and Chris and I went off on our own.

Was enjoying the break, chatting to Chris about football, when horrors, G and Melissa came in, arms wrapped around each other, walking so close you'd think they were velcroed together.

Nearly choked on my drink. Couldn't bear to stay a moment longer so just dashed out, leaving Chris without explanation. Went home in tears. Horrible day.

Had a packet of Jaffa Cakes and watched MTV all night, which cheered me up a bit but am still devastated, of course, as my life is meaningless without G.

WeDNeSDaY APRIL 19TH

Julian emailed Liz back saying he would need counselling to assist him in resolving his difficulties with his father and would Liz agree to help? He suggested Saturday evening. They could go for a pizza and have a therapy session at the same time. Liz said OK.

She loves pizza.

I don't fancy Julian myself but I do wish I had a boyfriend if only to forward his emails to my pals. Maybe I've spent too much time hankering after G and should look elsewhere but what fanciable guy is going to go for a skinny flat-chested brunette?

THURSDaY APRIL 20TH

Liz says I need to work on my self-esteem and has

given me exercises to perform three times a day. I have to stand in front of the mirror and say, 'You are absolutely gorgeous, you beautiful, sexy girl,' while caressing my body sensually. Don't ask who happened to enter my room during this procedure.

SaTURDaY APRIL 22ND

Stephanie and Liz both have dates so had to spend the entire evening with MnP and boyfriend. Seems like everyone is in a couple except me. Mind you, would rather die a bitter old maid than go out, or stay in, with someone like Graham.

SUNDaY APRIL 23RD
EASTER SUNDAY

Had chocolate eggs for breakfast, lunch and dinner. Delicious.

MONDaY APRIL 24TH

No spots at all this morning. So much for the chocolate/bad complexion link.

Liz came round to gossip about her date with

Stephanie's brother, although she said it was not a date but a counselling session over pizza. She advised Julian that the conflict with his father was probably due to unresolved Oedipus complex issues exacerbated by his parents' divorce.

According to Liz, all boys at some time secretly fancy their mum and wish their father would go away. If the father really does go away, for example after a divorce, the son is left feeling guilty and angry.

Julian said that all the talk of fancying his mum was putting him off his pizza but it didn't seem to put him off Liz as he's asked for another date (therapy appointment).

Liz refused a goodnight kiss, on the grounds of professional ethics, but agreed to a further appointment in order to explore Julian's psyche in more detail.

He certainly needs his head examined to put up with all this rubbish from Liz – must be bonkers about her.

TUESDAY APRIL 25TH

Chris phoned and suggested studying together at the library. Was so bored I agreed. Got quite a lot of work done and Chris helped me with my chemistry. Linda Robertson was there too. Apparently she's come every day in the hope of talking to him. As usual she was drawing me dirty looks as she still believes Chris is interested in me. Felt sorry for her really but someone should tell her how stupid and unattractive jealousy can be.

WEDNESDAY APRIL 26TH

Bumped into Melissa bloody Campbell at the shops today. She smiled and said 'Hi' as though nothing was wrong. Didn't even bother to try to be civil to her and scowled back. At least she wasn't with G. Hope he's dumped her.

SATURDAY APRIL 29TH

Awful day. Liz and Stephanie both had dates so once again I had to stay in with MNP and co.

Suppose I'll just have to take up embroidery, and buy a cat or something, except I can't sew and I'm allergic to cats.

Maybe I should become a nun then people will think my boyfriendless state is due to religious fervour instead of the fact that no one seems to fancy me. But then I guess I'd have to be a Catholic first, and thanks to Mr Dunn the only thing I know about Catholicism is stuff about the Spanish Inquisition which I don't think is going to impress the local priest as evidence of my desire for conversion.

Looks like I'll just have to put up with my fate as the only girl in the fourth year too ugly to get a date.

SUNDay APRIL 30TH

Fantastic day! Guess what? Melissa has dumped G!!!

Apparently Melissa had emailed her pal Louise about it and Louise forwarded the message to Anne, Sharon and Theresa, who sent it on to Veronica, Margaret, Catherine, Kylie, Susan, Eileen, Alison, Carol and Liz, who sent it to me.

In the email Melissa said that G was a complete tosser and she couldn't imagine what she ever saw in him. She said that she must have been bonkers to have gone out with him and thank God it was over. She berated her friends for allowing her to date such a prat, and said that next time she contemplated a relationship with anyone remotely resembling G, they were to lock her up until she'd come to her senses. She added that if G were the last male on earth after a nuclear holocaust she still wouldn't have him, and that if it came to a choice between a relationship with him and a giant two-headed mutant ant, the ant would win hands down, no contest.

Wonderful news. G is free again.

Liz asked, 'Doesn't Melissa's email tell you something?'

Of course it did. She obviously suspected G was going to chuck her so she got in first then made up all those spiteful comments.

Liz said she'd heard of love being blind but not deaf, dumb and totally nuts too.

Couldn't be bothered to be annoyed with Liz. Am just too ecstatically happy. G is free and I have hope again. Perhaps I'll catch him on the rebound. Happy day!

MONDAY MAY 1ST

Can't wait for school tomorrow when I'll see G again. Perhaps he'll still be upset about the break-up. I'll offer to comfort him and then he'll be so grateful he'll fall in love with me and finally realize I'm the one he wanted all along.

TUESDAY MAY 2ND

G didn't seem too upset at all so I won't be able to comfort him and get him on the rebound. Never mind, at least it proves he never really loved Melissa after all.

We had a fourth year assembly where all the teachers were banging on about how vitally important our Standard Grades are and how we now have less than two weeks to go before the start of the exams which will determine our whole future career and how they hoped we were all going to study really hard as the results will mean the difference between a successful, fulfilled, financially secure life and one of failure, drudgery and poverty but that we weren't to get anxious or nervous of course.

Yeah, right.

WeDNeSDaY MaY 3RD

Liz says Julian's dad is getting really impatient with him. He says Julian had to find a job soon or else.

Julian assured him that he had already sent off hundreds of applications and CVs but had had no reply and didn't his father know there was a recession on.

His dad said that there wasn't actually a recession on and that this was a booming period in the economy. He added that there might be a bust period for Julian in the near future if he didn't get his finger out, but that at least Julian would no longer have to feel guilty about accepting an allowance from a capitalist.

Julian said he got the message.

THURSDaY MaY 4TH

Ms Conner is running relaxation sessions in the hall at

lunch time to help pupils cope with stress in the run-up to the exams.

They are really fantastic. She plays womb music from a tape, which is a bit rubbish, but also burns lavender candles and gets us all to recline on beanbags whilst chanting calming words like serenity, peace and tranquillity. We can also invent our own mantras such as slouch, stay cool and Teletubbies.

It's all great fun and really works too. Afterwards our whole class fell asleep in maths. Mr Simmons was raging. We heard him tackle Ms Conner in the corridor. He told her that he didn't want his students relaxed as, in his opinion, they were far too complacent as it was. He told her that a bit of stress would be good for them; in fact, a lot more stress was exactly what was needed. He would thank her to discontinue her so-called relaxation sessions as of right then.

FRIDAY MAY 5TH

Ms Conner has extended her relaxation sessions to include any third years who may be experiencing pre-examination-year anxiety.

SaTURDaY MaY 6TH

Horrors! Julian has sent Liz an email and copied it to me and all Liz's friends. Somehow he has discovered that Liz forwards them to everyone and he says he wants to save her the bother.

Liz is mortified to be found out and immediately tackled Stephanie about it but she says she never tells her brother anything and Julian has probably sussed it because he's amazing with computers and can trace almost anything. He probably hacked into Liz's email.

Liz gave Julian a stern lecture on a person's inviolate right to privacy and confidentiality and has withdrawn all therapy sessions.

SUNDaY MaY 7TH

Julian is devastated by Liz's disapproval and has sent a grovelling apology to her, which she forwarded to everyone, but we've all decided his punishment should be extended.

MONDaY MaY 8TH

Julian has begged Liz to reconsider. He pointed out the dangers of an abrupt cessation of therapy and did she want to be responsible for his psychological collapse? He suggested a film on Friday followed by a counselling session and would she wear the black nylon plunge-neck top?

Liz said OK but it would have to be the low-cut scarlet stretch lace, which goes better with her leather mini.

Must be nice to have someone so mad keen on you. Wish I had a boyfriend like Liz's who would do anything just to spend time with me.

Chris came over tonight as I'd asked him to help with my science revision. He'd photocopied all the notes I'd missed and gave me his spare copies of past papers along with answers that he'd already done. He also explained some stuff to me, as he's brilliant at chemistry and biology. He's good at most things really but must say it does seem odd that he knows more about the menstrual cycle than I do.

Afterwards we ate the box of chocolates he'd brought round to cheer me up while I was studying.

Am getting really worried about the exams and so is everyone else except for Stephanie and G.

Stephanie hasn't got time to worry as she's too busy going on shopping expeditions, planning her holidays and maintaining her active sex life. Academic ambition is a totally alien idea to her.

G, on the other hand, is very ambitious. He says he is going to be a rich and famous footballer so he won't need any Standard Grades and he can't afford time for studying as he needs to concentrate on football practice.

I so admire G. Imagine knowing from such a young age exactly what you want and having the courage and conviction to follow your dream despite opposition from family and teachers who may be blind to your genius.

Mentioned this to Chris tonight but as usual he was unimpressed. He just said that the school team had to play a man down on Saturday because G hadn't bothered to turn up and that it's a well-known fact that G hardly ever manages to get out of bed for a morning match or practice.

Chris is all right but am afraid he is one of those people who cannot comprehend G's exceptional talent and sensitivity. No doubt G had a very good reason for his absence that morning. Hope he wasn't injured or unwell. Must ask him how he is tomorrow.

TUESDAY MAY 9TH

Plucked up courage and asked G how he was feeling then asked him why he hadn't made it to the match last Saturday. He laughed and just said that he'd had a bad hangover after he and a mate polished off two bottles of Buckie on the Friday night.

Feel privileged that G should feel able to talk about his personal weaknesses to me. Of course, nearly all exceptionally talented people have struggled with drink or drugs at some time in their lives – just look at all the rich and famous people who book into the Betty Ford Clinic or The Priory – maybe it's the price paid for genius. Of course, when we're finally together he will find the strength to conquer his personal demons and he'll tell everyone he owes everything to my steadfast love and support.

WEDNESDAY MAY 10TH

Liz is on yet another diet. This one is different in that it allows her to eat whatever she wants – there are no forbidden foods – and as much as she likes. The only catch is she can only eat before nine am – then she is not allowed any food until the following morning.

She had to get up at six o'clock this morning in order to prepare and consume enough to keep her going for the day. She had a slice of toast and a boiled egg, two pork chops with mashed potatoes, carrots and gravy, then sticky toffee pudding, a cup of tea, and three digestive biscuits.

She felt quite sick in maths first period but managed to keep going until lunch, when she fell asleep in the toilets. By home time she was quite recovered but ravenous again so tucked into fish and chips, followed by ice-cream and a packet of crisps.

Stephanie reckons Liz had got through about seven thousand calories by the end of the day. Some diet!

THURSDAY MAY 11TH

Stephanie has dumped her bin man for a construction worker she saw in Ingram Street last weekend.

She says she took one look at his tanned torso in low cut baggy jeans (which exposed a bit of firm bum) and fell instantly in love. She says he has a body to die for and we can all go to see him on Saturday.

FRIDAY MAY 12TH

Liz's dad is worried about her. He says Julian, at eighteen, is too old for her and she should find someone her own age. And yes, he knew that Julian was only three years older than Liz, but that boys learn a lot in those three years. He told her that the fact he was ten years older than her mother had nothing to do with it, as that was a different matter entirely.

Liz tried to reassure her dad – on her way out – by pointing out that Julian was not a boyfriend but a client. He said nothing more after that. Just stood on the doorstep gawping while Liz hurried off to her appointment.

SATURDAY MAY 13TH

Stephanie's new boyfriend is gorgeous. Some of the other guys working with him are pretty fit too. Liz, Stephanie and I went round to the building site to watch them work and we had a great time wolf whistling and shouting lewd suggestions.

They all looked a bit embarrassed and tried their best to ignore us while self-consciously pulling up their trousers to cover their bums properly. All except Stephanie's boyfriend Dave, who winked and called out that he'd see to her later.

Afterwards we went for a McDonald's and Stephanie told us that her dad is furious with Julian. Apparently her dad found a copy of Julian's CV. Hardly surprising he wasn't pleased. Stephanie showed us an extract.

Qualifications: None
Experience: None
Hobbies: Soft porn & recreational drugs
Ambitions: The overthrow of capitalist oppression
Membership of professional associations or clubs: Anarchist Radical Society for Extremists (ARSE), Bone-idle Underachievers and Misfits Society (BUMS)

Julian's allowance has been stopped.

SUNDAY MAY 14TH

Spent yesterday evening and all of today revising for my English exam tomorrow. Am very nervous as I really want to do well in this. My mum says just to do my best and that's all anyone can expect and my dad says I'll be fine.

But what if my best isn't good enough? What if I'm sick like Susan Cafferty last year, the one who spewed up over her essay? Or worse, I might faint in the hall during the interpretation paper, like Annette Smith did, and everyone would see my knickers if my skirt rode up.

Hers had a Paddington Bear picture on the front and she's never lived it down. Apparently they were her 'lucky knickers', prior to the fainting incident anyway.

Must make sure I've got a clean pair of plain white knickers for tomorrow, or better still, wear trousers.

MONDAY MAY 15TH

English went well, I think. Once I got started I was fine although the invigilator annoyed me by constantly pacing up and down the aisle in clackety shoes, occasionally stopping to peer at someone's work, then moving on with a superior, amused smile or a resigned shake of the head.

When we got out Ms Conner was waiting for us in the corridor to quiz us about how we got on.

She told one Higher pupil, who thought he had performed well, not to be too optimistic and to just wait and see. Her caution was caused by his assertion, 'I done OK, Miss.'

TUESDAY MAY 16TH

Spent the whole day and night revising for maths tomorrow. It is so hard and I'm scared I'll fail as I'm not very good at it. Mind you, I'm much better than Stephanie who is clueless but doesn't care.

She is particularly puzzled by algebra. Only last month she asked Mr Simmons, 'Why on earth would anyone want to count with letters?'

When he tried to explain she interrupted him to say, 'But if x equals seven why not just call it seven? I mean it says here,' and she pointed to the problem with a perfectly manicured finger, 'let x be seven. Well then, for goodness' sake, let it be seven and never mind the x.'

Mr Simmons told us all to get on with our work and spent the rest of the lesson perusing the Situations Vacant section of the newspaper. We noticed that he skipped over the education jobs without so much as a glance. Odd.

WEDNESDAY MAY 17TH

Maths this morning was hard but am hoping I might have scraped a pass. Stephanie had finished all she could do in just ten minutes then spent the rest of the time filing her nails and blowing kisses at the particularly crusty old invigilator.

Since none of us had an exam until Friday we went to Stephanie's after dinner. Her mum was out with Pierre so Julian poured us glasses of wine in lovely crystal glasses the size of small buckets. I felt so sophisticated and elegant sipping from mine that I didn't add any Coke even though it tasted awful.

Julian told us that he was now working in telesales. He'd agreed on Monday to take a job with a company called Funerals Direct. On his first day he was given a list of phone numbers for old people in the district and instructed to offer free burial plots if they agreed to book their funeral service with the company and make a small down payment.

Trouble was, the list was about ten years out of date and Julian discovered that most of them had already popped their clogs. Sometimes he would get a surviving son or daughter on the phone and would try to convince them to have a second, much improved funeral to commemorate their parent but most of them balked at the hassle of exhumation orders.

* * *

Later Julian took Liz off to his room to show her his new computer and get a spot of counselling. Yeah, right. From the giggles which emanated from next door, Stephanie and I reckoned that some professional ethics were definitely being breached.

Got home around eleven then suddenly realized that x was equal to 2y minus 3 not plus 3 as I'd written for question 5b part (ii).

Bollocks.

THURSDAY MAY 18TH

Biology tomorrow. Am finding the revision really hard going. I mean, who wants to know about the sex life of a daffodil? And I've studied the menstrual cycle until it's coming out my ears but I still don't understand it.

Dad says he knows all he needs to know about the menstrual cycle. He says that with three females in the house it means he only gets any peace about two days a month. The rest of the time, he maintains, he's tormented with someone or other flying off the flaming handle, bursting into soddin' tears or sulking in their rooms and – and this is what really buggering well gets him – always blaming him.

FRIDAY MAY 19TH

Biology wasn't too bad as most of what I'd studied came up. The biology teacher, Mr Quigley, asked us all afterwards how we got on and upon finding out how some of us tackled particular questions he said he wanted to clarify a few points.

He told us that asexual reproduction did indeed involve a single organism but had nothing to do with masturbation and that organism is spelt with a 'ni'. He also pointed out that although an erection is referred to in the vernacular as a 'boner', the male reproduction organ had, in fact, no bones and the penis was therefore not an example of a ball-and-socket joint.

Then he added that he'd been speaking to one of the invigilators at the exam – and here he glared at G, most unfairly I thought – and that he would like to know which joker drew the suspenders and stockings on the diagram of the female reproductive system.

With that, he walked off looking grim. Don't know why the teachers want to ask us about the exams after we've sat them. It just seems to depress them. Mr Simmons, the maths teacher, has been looking pretty cheerful lately though. Rumour has it he has placed a substantial bet on ours being the most stupid year ever presented for external exams in the history of the school and he feels confident of the outcome.

SaTURDaY MaY 20TH

Julian has been sacked. Bored with telesales, he volunteered to stand in for a hearse driver who was ill. He collected the coffin from the church after the funeral service and the procession of mourner cars followed him to the graveyard, where he literally lost the plot – that is, couldn't find the burial place.

After circling round for twenty minutes, respectfully followed by a cortege of at least thirty cars, he realized that he'd gone to the wrong graveyard.

Trying to make up for lost time he sped off, screeching for the exit at a rate of knots, then took to the motorway pursued by the funeral procession.

They were all doing at least eighty-five miles per hour when they were pulled up by the traffic police. Julian tried to talk his way out of it, pleading an emergency, but the police weren't buying any of it, reasonably pointing out that his passenger wasn't in a hurry.

Everyone involved, including the minister and all the grieving relatives, received hefty fines. Only the corpse got off with a warning. Our police force is so witty. Not.

SUNDaY MaY 21ST

History tomorrow. Does that make sense? Too tired to think about it now. Will these exams ever end?

MONDAY MAY 22ND

Following our history exam our teacher pointed out the following to us. One, the American War of Independence took place before, not after, the Second World War and the Americans, not the British, won.

And two, on the subject of the Second World War: Poland did not invade Germany. Mussolini was not on our side. Countries on our side were called Allies not 'goodies', and the enemy should not be referred to as 'fascist bastards' in a history essay no matter what anyone's grandad says.

Later we saw him hand over a tenner to Mr Simmons saying there was no point in waiting for the results in August and he wanted to concede now.

TUESDAY MAY 23RD

French tomorrow.

The French must be mental. I mean, why give everything a gender, even tables and chairs? It's mad. Might not be so bad if the choice of gender made any sense but when you get feminine beards and masculine bras it's time to give up trying to make any sense of things.

Wish I were Stephanie. She's brilliant at French

because of all her holidays in the south of France and shopping trips to Paris.

weDNeSDaY maY 24TH

Mrs Valentine met us before the exam to give us a brief, determinedly cheerful pep talk. With a bright orange lip-sticked smile she wished us good luck and waved us off as we shuffled miserably into the exam hall. *'Bonne chance, mes enfants. À bientôt.'*

Yeah right.

When we filed out at the end Mrs Valentine was waiting for us, fixed orange grin still in place.

After we told her how we got on she was seen wandering up and down the corridors muttering to herself, *'Mon Dieu. Quels imbéciles! Idiots! Merde. Merde. Merde.'*

Art tomorrow but at least I don't have to study for that.

THURSDaY maY 25TH

Art was OK. We had a still life of a wine bottle and bowl of fruit to paint and I think mine turned out quite well.

The only hitch was that when we returned to our work after a fifteen-minute toilet break someone had eaten one of the apples and a banana, leaving just the core and banana skin behind.

The invigilator went mad, wildly threatening to call the police and have the thief brought to justice. In the end someone donated an apple from their packed lunch and we just put the banana skin together again and returned it to the bowl.

It was a bit of a nuisance as the replacement apple was green, whereas the original had been red, and I'd already coloured in half of mine but it looked OK in the end. Everyone's banana looked a bit sad and flaccid though.

FRIDAY MAY 26TH

Last exam was chemistry. Went OK I think. Anyway, it's all over. Hooray!

It being our final exam, Stephanie, Liz, Chris and I decided to go to Burger King straight after as a treat. Guess who was there? G! And he came and sat at our table! And he talked to me!!! Well, he talked to all of us in general but I think he looked at me more.

Liz suggested we all go out to see a film at the Odeon tonight. She said it was a romantic comedy and supposed to be very good.

Unfortunately G said that he wasn't interested in chick flicks but the rest of us decided to go.

As it turned out, though, only Chris and me went.

Liz called to say that she really needed to spring clean her room as it was a tip. Strange. Liz's room is always a tip but she's never felt the need to clean it before, especially not on a Friday night. Maybe the stress of the exams is finally catching up with her and causing her to act so out of character.

Then Stephanie phoned to say she really needed to catch up with some studying. Weird. Stephanie never studies and the exams are finished. Beginning to think my mum is right about my friends. They are a peculiar lot.

The film was great. It was about this girl who is madly in love with a guy who everyone but her can see is a useless tosser and completely wrong for her. Meanwhile she ignores this gorgeous guy who is also a fantastic person and totally devoted to her. Obviously in the end she realizes what a waste of space the tosser is and falls head over heels for Mr Gorgeous.

Really enjoyed the story even if it was a bit unbelievable. Can't imagine any real person being as daft as the girl in the movie.

Afterwards Chris saw me home even though he would have been better getting off a stop earlier for his place. I keep telling him not to bother walking me right to my door but he always insists. He can be so pig-headed.

MONDaY MaY 29TH

Late for school as I couldn't get into the bathroom due to MNP throwing up. Again. Don't know what's up with her. Stephanie says she's probably got a bug but Liz suggested that MNP might be bulimic and asked if she had lost any weight recently.

Now that I come to think about it, despite all the vomiting, she's actually put on a few pounds but mostly around the boobs, lucky thing. Personally I think it's due to the disgusting stuff she's eating these days. She seems to have acquired a taste for porridge with beetroot and has it for breakfast, lunch and dinner. No wonder she's sick all the time.

TUeSDaY MaY 30TH

Mum asked if anyone had noticed anything different about her today. We all tensed up, knowing this was some sort of test and there would be hell to pay if we failed.

Dad kicked off with: had she had her hair done and didn't it really suit her? MNP said she really liked Mum's top and was it a new one? However, I had spotted the leaflet Mum was carrying and fortunately am pretty good at reading upside down, even from a distance, so hit the jackpot with, 'Wow, Mum, you look at least ten years younger today.'

Apparently Mum had visited the beautician's, which had a special offer on a revolutionary new facial. The treatment used ingredients that 'combined the ancient secrets of Egyptian embalmers with the latest cutting-edge scientific advances to emerge from NASA researchers'.

Yeah, right.

And it was only sixty-five pounds, or three hundred and sixty for a course of six. Mum had booked the course of six, thereby 'saving' thirty pounds.

WEDNESDAY MAY 31ST

Can't believe it. MNP is pregnant!

We were all sitting at dinner tonight, MNP having her usual porridge and beetroot mix, while the rest of us were tucking into gammon and chips, when suddenly MNP asked if anyone had noticed anything different about her lately.

Wasn't going to get into all that again, not for MNP anyway, so I just said, yes, she was getting fat and could I have her pink shirt as it was too tight for her now?

Next thing I knew she'd burst into tears and said, 'I'm pregnant, you idiot.'

After that it was pandemonium. Mum just went mental, screeching like a deranged howler monkey. How

113

could MNP do this to her? Hadn't she any decency at all? No one must find out about this and oh, the shame of it.

Dad said, 'Steady on, Moira. We aren't living in the Dark Ages for God's sake. Girls don't have to go drowning themselves in the bloody mill pond when they get up the duff any more.'

'Mill pond my arse,' screamed Mum. 'You just don't get it, do you? That eejit of a daughter' – and here she glared at MNP – 'is going to make me a . . . make me a . . .'

'Granny,' I finished.

THURSDAY JUNE 1ST

Wonder if I should ask about the pink shirt again. Probably not.

The house is still in uproar. Mum has taken to her room and won't come out, even to eat. She refuses to speak to anyone, except to me, to tell me to buy her some fags. Had to try three shops before finding one that would sell them to me. Have a mother who sends me out to break the law. Great.

Graham came over. He told Dad that he intends to stand by MNP. He says that after the baby is born they will find a place to live, then get married the following year when he is due to be promoted.

Dad said something about baby, house, then wedding, weren't they doing things arse backwards?

Graham laughed dutifully. Dad said he wasn't trying to be funny and to wipe the smirk off his face before Dad wiped it off for him.

FRIDAY JUNE 2ND

Have discovered that the accident happened when MNP and Graham unexpectedly ran out of condoms and decided to chance it. Keep thinking about G using them as balloons at my party in March. Maybe if I hadn't had the party and G hadn't taken all the condoms then MNP wouldn't be having a baby.

Don't think I'll mention these musings to Mum.

SATURDAY JUNE 3RD

My dad has allowed Graham to stay overnight for the first time. Suppose it's because he's now a future in-law. He has to sleep on the sofa in the living room though, which seems a bit daft to me. He might as well sleep with MNP. The damage has already been done after all. Talk about locking the stable doors after the horse has bolted.

Mum is still in her room. Since no one else can cook we've been living off fish and chips and takeaway Chinese, which is great. We pass Mum's share in to her and she leaves the remains outside the door when she's finished.

Dad has tried to persuade her to come out but so far there hasn't been any response other than a suggestion that he should away and boil his head. Charming.

Am so looking forward to going to Paris on Monday. Hope Mum will have got over this granny thing by the time I get back.

MONDAY JUNE 5TH

Shouted goodbye to Mum through the bedroom door but was told to bugger off, didn't I realize it was only six o'clock and she had a hangover? Charming. Serves her right if my plane crashes and she is tortured with guilt for ever at the thought of her last words to me.

Dad drove me to the airport then carried my case to the check-in queue. Spotted G right away. He was near the front looking gorgeous in loose jeans and a black shirt.

Joined the end of the line along with Liz and Chris who'd been looking for me. Dad said goodbye and then he totally embarrassed me by kissing me on the forehead. Don't think G saw it, thank God.

No one could find Stephanie until Mr Simmons spotted her waiting in the first-class queue by mistake and went over to re-direct her. She handed him her Gucci luggage to carry for her and, without a backward glance, marched off to join us.

Mr Simmons caught up with her and told her that he wasn't her flunky, and if she ever tried anything like that again he would personally tell her where to stick her overpriced piece of rampant consumerism and did she understand him?

Stephanie said that she did.

Our other minders were Ms Conner who can speak French too, Miss McElwee and Mr Dunn. Everyone knows Mr Dunn has had to purchase his own fare plus take a week of unpaid leave. It's perfectly obvious he's just come along because he fancies the pants off Ms Conner. He hasn't a hope, of course. Someone should tell him he's just wasting his time but I don't suppose he'd listen. What an idiot.

After checking in, Liz and I went off to buy essentials that Stephanie told us were unavailable in France. We got Irn Bru, proper British sweets and magazines. Liz had already smuggled potato scones, square sausages and baked beans in her suitcase.

Saw G at the airport pharmacy buying condoms and popping one in his shirt pocket, which made me blush. *If only.*

When it was time to board Ms Conner spotted the condom, which was partially sticking out of his pocket and so quite visible (am sure this was an oversight on G's part but Stephanie says not), and questioned him about it. Ms Conner is usually OK but I really think this constituted an invasion of privacy.

Anyway, G was quite unfazed by her. He is *so* sophisticated. He told her that he believed in being responsible and taking steps to avoid the spread of disease or unwanted pregnancy.

Ms Conner told him not to be so silly. She said that protection was only required when there were two people involved in a sex act and that therefore he had no need of prophylactics. Everyone except G and me thought this remark was hilarious and laughed like deranged hyenas but I didn't think it was funny at all.

Not that G let it bother him. On the plane he engaged in some witty repartee with the air hostesses – or trolley dollies, as he laughingly called them, telling them that they weren't bad looking but not nearly as sexy as the ones on Aer Lingus.

They took this in good part, enjoying his light-hearted banter and smiling throughout, and the hostess who accidentally let the ice bucket fall on his lap couldn't have been more apologetic. Especially on the second occasion.

Arrived at Charles de Gaulle airport.

Really weird to hear all these French people actually talking in French, apparently without being in the least embarrassed about their *Pink Panther* accent. Tried to pick out what they were saying but everyone was talking far too quickly. Don't see why they all have to prattle on at such a rate.

Took nearly an hour to get to our hotel in the Latin Quarter. Would have taken much longer if we hadn't had a maniacal coach driver who largely ignored the city traffic and seemed to drive with his eyes shut in the expectation that every other vehicle would make way for us. I found it pretty scary but Stephanie assured us that it was the only way to drive in Paris.

Liz, Stephanie and I are sharing a room. Liz and I think it's really nice but Stephanie kept complaining about there being no room service, satellite TV, or minibar. We told her to can it.

But the best thing is G is right next door to us! Have bagged the bed next to the wall separating his room from mine. We'll be practically sleeping together! Chris, Ian and Gary are sharing G's room. None of G's friends are on the trip so I suppose he won't mind sharing with Chris's lot. Hope they make sure G has got enough wardrobe space and a comfortable bed. Maybe I should offer him the use of some of mine. Wardrobe space, that is, not bed. Ha ha!

Miss McElwee is not happy about the arrangements. She'd asked the manager to put the boys and girls on separate floors but he'd just shrugged his shoulders and said that it was, '*Trop difficile, madame.*' When she persisted he replied, '*Impossible, je regrette,*' then turned his back on her. He gave us a little smile and wink, though, before walking off.

We had lunch at the hotel before Mrs Valentine took us on an orientation expedition around the immediate neighbourhood. It looks a great area with loads of shops and cafés. Am so excited. Imagine, nearly a whole week in Paris with G. Well, G and around forty others, but still.

Afterwards we went back and finished unpacking.

Mrs Valentine said we could have dinner at the hotel or go out by ourselves but we had to be back by ten. Of course everyone went out to the McDonald's we'd spotted on the orientation trip but Mrs Valentine was ahead of us.

She stood barring the entrance and told us that there was no way she would allow us to come to the gourmet capital of the world only to eat at McDonald's. Then she split us into smaller groups and chased us away.

Found a café which served cheap *pommes frites* and Stephanie persuaded Liz and me to try the *moules*. Actually they were very tasty. Maybe Mrs Valentine has a point. Afterwards we went to a brasserie, where we were served wine with no questions asked. Brilliant.

Toilets not too brilliant. Couldn't believe it at first when I tried to use the facilities in the brasserie. I thought maybe some vandals had stolen the WC for a laugh but then Stephanie shouted through the door that I was supposed to squat on the floor tiles and pee into the hole in the middle. So much for Parisian chic.

Liz thought it was a hoot when I told her. She took her camera off to the toilet to record it for posterity then returned asking loudly for a model. Stephanie obliged on condition she got a copy of the photo.

The French customers looked at us as if we were nuts, muttering stuff like '*Les touristes sont des imbéciles stupides.*' Even I understood that one. They've got a nerve. We're not the ones with the absolutely bogging toilets, after all.

It was a nuisance having to go back at ten but we knew Miss McElwee would be waiting for us in the foyer. She made it clear that she would be staying there indefinitely to make sure we didn't try to slip out again.

This was very inconvenient as it meant we all had to climb off the balcony at the back and there was a six-metre drop at the end. It's a wonder no one broke an ankle.

Chris joined us, along with Ian and Gary, then G asked to come along! Was furious with the other boys when they said no at first and I made it clear that if G didn't come, then no one would, so Chris said OK.

We went for a few more glasses of wine then made our way back around midnight. Fortunately Miss McElwee had gone off to bed so we didn't need to climb in around the back, which was just as well as we were all a bit tipsy.

Am writing the last bit of this in bed only a wall away from G. Well, actually, not quite. Have discovered that the next-door toilet adjoins our room and the walls must be rather thin because I can hear the sound of flushing and other intimate noises. Still, just two walls and a toilet away from G. Have never been happier in my life.

TUESDAY JUNE 6TH

Walked to the Eiffel Tower this morning, which turned out to be no big deal. There didn't seem to be much to do there once we'd been up and down it. Stephanie had managed to dodge the trip, feigning illness, and had gone shopping in the Champs-Élysées instead.

She joined us in the afternoon for a tour of the Sacré-Coeur and lunch in Montmartre. It was a gloriously sunny day and the atmosphere in Montmartre was great. It was full of street artists, musicians and noisy cafés.

Spotted G sitting at an outside table and persuaded Liz and Stephanie to stop for a Coke there. We were seated just two tables away from him but he appeared not to notice us. He had his eyes on a group of very pretty French girls.

Eventually he went over to them and, using a phrase he'd picked up from an old pop song, said, '*Voulez-vous coucher avec moi?*'

This means, would you like to go to bed with me, and of course, G was just being witty but the girls turned out to have no sense of humour at all. One of them answered with a torrent of French, which I couldn't understand, but judging from her tone and furious expression, her meaning was not very nice.

Another did reply in – very poor in my opinion – English to say: 'Peess off, you leetle, how you say . . . er, tosser.'

We had dinner at the hotel this time to save money as meals are included then went out in the evening again. Some of the French boys are really nice and if I wasn't committed to G I would find them very fanciable, especially when they call me Mademoiselle and ask me if I have a light, which seems to be the usual way of striking up conversation.

Nearly everyone smokes here. The females never seem to eat anything and only drink black coffee but they get through a lot of fags which smell worse than my mum's. Liz said, a bit nastily I thought, that this is how they stay so slim.

Miss McElwee was waiting for us at ten, and after midnight, when we got back for the second time, she was still guarding the entrance, so we had to climb around the back twice. Wish she'd get a life before someone gets injured.

WEDNESDAY JUNE 7TH

Spent the whole day at the Louvre today. Could have spent a week. It is absolutely awesome.

Particularly loved the Italian section. Totally gobsmacked by the most beautiful paintings I've ever seen. Mind you, I think I'd have been really pissed off if I were Italian as the French seem to have got their hands on all their best art. They've even got the *Mona Lisa*.

Everything was going really well until Stephanie annoyed Miss McElwee by pretending to intimately caress a statue of a naked man. Everyone else in the enormous crowded hall thought her act was hilarious but Mrs

Valentine hissed at her to stop her disgraceful display immediately.

However, Stephanie was unrepentant, telling Miss McElwee not to get her knickers in a twist because it wasn't as though she were miming fellatio or anything. She was grounded on the spot.

Then Liz waded in to defend Stephanie and offered Miss McElwee therapy to overcome her repressive tendencies, whereupon she was grounded too.

All I did was to ask what fellatio was. Thought my grounding was unfair as I genuinely didn't know, although I do now after Stephanie's frank, detailed and public explanation.

Had to spend the entire evening in possibly the most romantic city in Europe, stuck in a hotel room with Stephanie and Liz. Cheered up when Chris smuggled us in some cheese, baguettes and wine, however.

Stephanie grabbed him and gave him a huge kiss right on the mouth to thank him. He seemed a bit flustered at first but rallied to demand the same token of gratitude from Liz and me.

Liz immediately hugged him and planted a slobbery kiss on his lips but I felt a bit shy, which is odd really as I've known him longer than anyone, and it would look daft to go all girly and refuse.

In the end Chris solved the problem by taking me in his arms and kissing me. It seemed to go on for a long time and I got this really weird but very pleasant fluttery sensation in my stomach. When he let me go I felt kind of disappointed somehow, as though I wanted to stay as we were just a bit longer.

Then Chris was asking: 'Are you OK, Kelly Ann?'

And I said, "Course, but you better run before old McElwee comes to check on us.'

Spent the rest of the evening getting mildly drunk on the wine and stuffing ourselves with the cheese and baguettes but I was feeling a bit tetchy and restless. Eventually Stephanie asked what was wrong with me. Didn't really know myself, but said I supposed I wished G would kiss me the way Chris did tonight.

I expected a smart, sarcastic response but instead Stephanie went all serious and said, 'Kelly Ann, you may or may not one day go out with G but he will never, ever kiss you the way Chris did tonight.'

Stephanie is the first person ever to say that I might possibly one day go out with G. Am so excited!

THURSDAY JUNE 8TH

Awful day.

Woke up with really painful cramp due to start of my period and have developed an enormous spot the size of a witch's wart on the end of my chin. Paracetamol failed to help so couldn't go to Versailles with the rest and had to stay in the hotel.

Miss McElwee told everyone at breakfast that I wouldn't be going because I had a stomach upset but Ms Conner corrected her by publicly announcing that I was suffering from painful menses.

She added that she refused to collude with the sexist notion that a female's monthly bleed was a shameful secret to be hidden from society. This was, she said, an idea fostered by men for centuries and had its origins in their irrational fear of women's powerful reproductive capacity and that she, for one, was no longer prepared to pander to male weaknesses.

Great, now the whole world knows I have my period! Am totally mortified. Thanks a bunch, Ms Conner.

Everyone had an absolutely fabulous time at Versailles. Am so pleased for them. Not.

FRIDAY JUNE 9TH

Last full day in Paris as we travel back tomorrow. We are being allowed to spend it as we please, hurrah! And can stay out until ten-thirty. Wow!

Decided to use the Métro to get to as many different Paris destinations as possible. Suppose the buses would have been more fun but we were scared of getting lost and it's impossible for anyone, even the most stupid person, to get lost on the Métro.

So Liz, Stephanie and I spent the day like moles,

diving down into the bowels of the earth for short periods of time then re-emerging to explore the sights, sounds and smells of Paris.

What a gorgeous place. Even, the *names* of their streets and monuments sound beautiful; L'Etoile, L'Arc de Triomphe, Rue de la Fayette, Champs Élysées, Sacré-Coeur. Hate to seem disloyal but it beats Sauchiehall Street or Sighthill any day.

Arranged to meet the boys, Chris, Gary, Ian and – last but not least of course – G, at a café in Montmartre for lunch.

G wasn't there. Apparently he had split from the others to go and look at the Pigalle area and everyone was annoyed with me for insisting we postpone lunch until he arrived.

We sat at an outside table and ordered drinks while we perused the menu and salivated over the sight of the other customers eating. G was only around an hour late, explaining that he'd got lost after taking several wrong Métro lines, or the right lines but the wrong direction, he wasn't sure.

We were all starving by this time so ordered lunch straight away. While we were waiting for our food, G spotted pretty French twin girls at a nearby table and tried to strike up a conversation with them. He asked them if they fancied a '*ménage à trois*' but they proved yet again that Parisians have no sense of humour by taking offence at G's light-hearted icebreaker.

Their boyfriends were even less amused when they returned and so aggressive in fact that we all had to leave quickly without our lunch. Poor G.

For our last night in Paris we planned to go out with the boys and get very drunk. Was so disappointed to hear that G wouldn't be able to join us as he was feeling a bit under the weather. Offered to stay and look after him but Ian said that G really needed rest and quiet so finally I agreed to go without him.

We all managed to get suitably inebriated but not, as we discovered later, as totally rat-arsed as others.

Around midnight, we were walking back to the hotel when we spotted Ms Conner swaying drunkenly along the street beside Mr Dunn, who had one arm slung supportively around her waist, whilst the other was swinging an open bottle of wine. But it was the sight of Mr Simmons and Mrs Valentine on the other side of the road, sharing a passionate kiss, that had us totally gobsmacked, especially since they are both married – and not to each other.

Gary wolf-whistled at them and they broke apart immediately, then shouted over something about us being out after curfew, but we just stared confidently back as we reckoned we had more on them than they did on us.

Later Ian and Gary confessed that G had not been unwell.

They had stripped him and locked him in the toilet in retaliation for spoiling their lunch and doing other annoying stuff like hogging the bathroom for hours on end.

Thought it was unfair of Gary and Ian to object to a person being particular about their personal hygiene and said so.

Gary said, 'Personal hygiene, I don't think so.' He claimed that G spent hours locked in the toilet looking at the dirty French magazines he'd bought.

This was rubbish, of course. No doubt they had mistaken some book on art, which happened to have a few nudes, for a dirty magazine. This was pretty typical of Gary and Ian, but must say I had expected better of Chris.

Chris assured me that he'd had nothing to do with G's physical incarceration. He admitted that he had happened to mention earlier in the evening that the toilet door could be locked from the outside and so it was possible someone could be accidentally imprisoned therein. However, he said he'd made plain his level of disapproval for his friends' subsequent actions.

Was somewhat mollified by Chris's explanation but thought he might have done more to protect G. As for Gary and Ian, I can only assume, as I said to Liz and Stephanie, that they are jealous of G's sparkling personality and his certain *je ne sais quoi*.

Liz replied, rather sarcastically as usual, 'Yeah right, *je ne sais quoi* either.'

Stephanie just said, 'Bollocks.'

Charming.

SaTURDaY JUNe 10TH

Was sad to leave Paris as I had a great time there and had grown fond of pommes frites and moules, not to mention Liz's favourite, croissants and hot chocolate, but had run out of Irn Bru so perhaps it was time to go.

Everyone was hungover and quiet on the journey except Miss McElwee. Arrived at Glasgow ten minutes early so we were soon gathered at the airport arrivals, waiting to be picked up by our respective parents and conscious that no one had remembered to send postcards to them.

Had managed to manoeuvre myself so that I was standing beside G. After all, I would not be able to see him again until Monday. After nearly a whole week sleeping next to him, sort of, I was missing him already.

Was scanning the airport trying to find my dad when G nudged me and said, 'Hey, Kelly Ann, look at that sad old slapper over there.'

Looked in the direction of his smirk and could see what he meant. Even though her face was partly hidden beneath baseball cap and dark glasses it was obvious she was well past thirty yet she was dressed like a teenage groupie.

She wore a crotch-skimming, fake leather skirt that exposed dimpled thighs and a shocking pink sequinned boob tube that miserably failed to support her rather droopy breasts. What a sight!

G was looking at her and sniggering but I told him to shut up as she was headed in our direction and might hear him.

Next thing I knew she came right up to me and started talking. She said, 'How was your trip, Kelly Ann?'

Mum!!!

SUNDAY JUNE 11TH

Am totally mortified. Mum has gone mad.

Dad says she's been like this since I left. He says she can't stand the thought of becoming a granny, as it makes her feel like she's completely past it. She won't talk about MNP's pregnancy and just spends all her time in her room playing loud rap music and trying on outlandishly youthful clothes.

Last night she refused to go to their normal local and insisted she and Dad went out clubbing. Dad told her she must be bloody joking and he wasn't prepared to be a laughing stock or a sleazy old perve cruising bars meant for people half their age.

She told him that she wasn't dead yet and that if he thought she was going to spend the rest of her life crocheting tea cosies he could think again.

He replied, 'Crochet, my arse.' He went on to tell her that she had never been able to crochet, knit, sew or perform a single domestic task well in their entire marriage. He said that he didn't mind all that but he would not and could not stand her swanning around pretending to be Britney bloody Spears for God's sake and that she needed to get a grip.

No one said anything after that and Mum went out by herself.

MONDAY JUNE 12TH

Am so humiliated. Had to face school today after everyone seeing Mum at the airport.

Talked to Chris about it while we were waiting to go into maths after break. He told me not to worry. He said that – get this – Mum was a nice-looking woman for her age and that, although he didn't think her outfit was flattering, it was up to her what she chose to wear and it wasn't anyone else's business.

G overheard his comment about my mum being nice looking and wound Chris up a bit, saying, 'Bloody hell, don't tell me you fancy the mum as well.'

Suppose G must think Chris is interested in me as more than just a pal because he said 'as well'. But I remembered what Stephanie had said about boys fancying people that other boys want so I didn't bother to correct him. Didn't have time anyway as Chris had pushed G up against the wall and offered to take him outside and 'beat the crap out of him' so I had to calm Chris down before he lost his temper totally.

Don't know why Chris can't get on with G. After all, he must know how much I like and admire G.

Moaned to Stephanie and Liz about my mum at lunch time. It's OK for Chris to say not to worry but it isn't his mother who's making a total show of herself.

Stephanie says it's just a phase and Mum will grow out of it but Liz thinks she needs counselling to navigate this period of her life and come to terms with the ageing process.

Was so desperate that I asked Liz to try it but she told me I had to be kidding. She said she wouldn't attempt such a dangerous mission even if she were a suicidal masochist on a downer. No way.

Suppose I'll just have to hope Stephanie is right and that Mum will grow out of it.

On my return home I could hear music blasting from our house a block away, some heavy metal rock stuff, I think. Got in and shouted up the stairs for her to turn that racket off but she ignored me.

When she finally sashayed down around dinner time she had on banana-yellow Lycra trousers cut very low on the hips, and a fluorescent orange tank top which barely reached the top of her ribcage, so exposing an acre of midriff and a newly pierced navel.

Dad asked her if she'd suddenly gone colour blind as well as nuts but Mum ignored him, saying to me:

'Tell your father he's a boring old fart.'

'Tell your mother being a boring old fart is better than looking like a tart on LSD.'

'Ask your father who he's calling a tart?'

'Tell your mother if the bloody shoe fits. Not that anything else she's got on does, mind you.'

Went upstairs and left them to it. Sometimes wonder what they'd do if I actually did what they asked and repeated the insults to them. Decided not to experiment with that idea tonight.

TUESDAY JUNE 13TH

Went over to Liz's tonight to avoid the poisoned atmosphere at home not to mention the awful loud music.

Liz is on a post holiday de-tox diet which means she can only consume bottled mineral water and fruit juices. When I arrived she was applying a honey and porridge face pack and invited me to try it, which I did.

Liz explained that the diet would purify her body on the inside by flushing out toxins in her blood, kidneys and liver, and the face pack would exfoliate and cleanse her skin on the outside.

However, after a few minutes Liz's hunger got the better of her and she started licking the paste from around her lip area even before it had dried.

She decided that perhaps she needed to eat just a little grain product to 'counteract the acidity of her fruit juice regime as well as to regain inner harmony and balance'.

We went down to the kitchen where Liz made six slices of thick toast, each one slathered with butter that dripped down our chins as we ate. Delicious.

Later we chatted as Liz texted Julian. Texting in no way interfered with the smooth flow of conversation as Liz is quite capable of punching out messages on her mobile without ever looking at the keypad, and simultaneously discussing whether Mr Dunn was ever going to get anywhere with Ms Conner. We decided his chances were about equal to those of Scotland winning the World Cup.

Thought sadly of Mum. Even if she didn't look so old her inability to send or receive even one text message would give her age away instantly. Why can't she see that?

WEDNESDAY JUNE 14TH

Begged Dad yet again for a mobile phone but got the same old excuses. Didn't I know that they might fry the brain and were especially dangerous for young people?

Told him that Stephanie had offered to give me her old one for free and that I would buy phone cards so that I wouldn't be running up a bill and he said OK then.

So much for the concerns about my health. Seems it's all right for me to get brain cancer just so long as it doesn't cost anything. Typical.

SaTURDaY JUNe 17TH

Liz is seeing Julian, and Stephanie has a date with her construction worker, Dave, tonight. Dad has reluctantly agreed to go to clubbing with Mum instead of to their local so am stuck in with pregnant MNP and Graham. Great.

They showed me a scan picture of the baby. It was gross. A spooky white apparition, with a face like the painting of *The Scream*, on a black background. Scary! But they were cooing over it like it was a photo of a proper baby on a Mothercare advert, and asking me what I thought and wasn't he or she just gorgeous.

Managed to mumble something about it being awesome or some such.

Wonder if my whole family has gone nuts!

SUNDAY JUNE 18TH

Mum was barred from The Hut nightclub even before she got in. Apparently the bouncers outside were checking IDs to ensure that no one under twenty-one tried to enter. When Mum proffered hers for examination she was told that it wouldn't be necessary as they didn't do concession rates for pensioners.

Mum called the bouncer a cheeky bugger and tried to knee him in the groin so the manager was called to see Mum and Dad off the premises and tell them not to darken the doors of his prestigious club again.

MONDAY JUNE 19TH

Mum and Dad had yet another argument, this time about the summer holidays. Mum wants to go back to Spain but Dad wants to tour Cornwall and Devon where we used to holiday when MNP and me were kids.

Mum says she wants sun, sea and sangria in Ibiza, not cream teas, pasties and double bingo sessions in bloody Cornwall and Devon.

Dad says there's no way he's going to Ibiza to watch her making a mug of herself trying to infiltrate the 18–30 clubs.

Mum says she's not dead yet and even if she were she'd still be going to Ibiza and he'd better just get used to it.

Dad says over his dead body, and Mum says that's fine with her.

Pretty morbid talk for a summer holiday if you ask me. But no one does.

It will be Liz's sixteenth birthday on Saturday, so she will then legally be allowed to have sex and a cigarette afterwards, but not a drink beforehand to get her in the mood.

TUESDAY JUNE 20TH

Liz is having her birthday do at Pizza Hut but has so far refused to invite G or any of his 'dodgy' friends. Begged and pleaded until Liz reluctantly gave in.

WEDNESDAY JUNE 21ST

G says he can come!!!

THURSDAY JUNE 22ND

Looked through my wardrobe for something to wear only to find Mum has 'borrowed' nearly all my clothes.

They now stink of cigarette smoke, and some have

been altered to make the hemlines shorter, neckline lower, and everything tighter.

It can't be right when your mother dresses even more tackily than you do.

FRIDAY JUNE 23RD

Stephanie lent me a silk spaghetti strap top and a fine suede short skirt. Must say I looked really good. Asked her if she thought G would fancy me now but she just muttered something about hoping her good deed wouldn't backfire.

Am so excited. Can't wait for tomorrow.

SATURDAY JUNE 24TH

G didn't turn up.

Had a pretty boring night. Tried to cheer myself up by eating five pieces of pizza, two bowls of chips and a chocolate ice-cream dessert. Almost as much as Liz on one of her diets, in fact, but nothing helped.

Finally left at half past ten. Don't think Chris could have enjoyed the night much either as he left at the same time and walked me home.

SUNDay JUNe 25TH

Fantastic day. Guess what? Heard that G had actually turned up later and asked where I was. He actually noticed I wasn't there! Am sure this is real progress but Liz says that's rubbish and he was probably just looking for someone to borrow money from. She has also suggested that I have bipolar disorder (which apparently means I'm a bit moody) and need intensive counselling, which she would be happy to provide for a modest fee. Told Liz to stick her bipolar disorder, her counselling and her fee. But was just too excited and happy to be really annoyed with her.

MONDay JUNe 26TH

Awful day. Mum and Dad had another horrific argument. Mum says she's booked a holiday in Ibiza for July with her divorced pal, Barbara.

Dad says over his dead body is she going to bloody Ibiza with that cheap tart and Mum says that's fine by her, and that by the way Barbara is not a cheap tart but just a woman who's not forgotten how to enjoy herself, like Mum's done since marrying Dad and more's the bloody pity.

Then Dad said to go then and see if he cared and Mum said, fine, she'd do just that.

Suppose there won't be a family holiday this year after all then. Probably just as well.

TUESDAY JUNE 27TH

Had to go shopping with Mum to help her choose stuff for her holiday. Tried to steer her to more mature places like Littlewoods and Marks and Spencer but no luck. She insisted on going to places where Liz and I might shop and I had to spend most of the day trying to shield her from view in the communal changing rooms.

Awful day. Don't even ask about the bikini shopping.

THURSDAY JUNE 29TH

Second last day of school. Free periods nearly all day. It was great at first but must say I was getting bored with playing cards, charades, hangman and ludo, so when we had English last thing and Ms Conner told us she would be reading some poetry to us I was almost relieved.

That is, until the subjects of the verses became clear. They were all what Ms Conner described as 'Vagina Monologues'. Couldn't believe it! Some mad females wittering on about their private parts. Was so embarrassed.

Ms Conner said it was important to redress the

imbalance of this hitherto phallocentric society. Yeah, right. Can't see guys writing monologues about their private bits, for God's sake.

G sniggered, Chris looked uncomfortable, and even the unshockable Stephanie was a bit taken aback.

According to Ms Conner these monologues were all about female empowerment. Empowerment, my arse. All us girls skulked out of the class feeling like walking vaginas.

Thank God there's no English tomorrow.

FRIDAY JUNE 30TH

Last day and just a morning at that. Now free at last but am going to miss G soooo much.

Went home at lunch time and helped Mum pack for her holiday. Her friend arrived around two o'clock and they both started drinking rum and Coke and singing 'Viva España' to get themselves in the mood for their trip.

Barbara's hair was hennaed an unnatural orange hue. Fake tan streaked unevenly across her thin face, crepey chest and skinny legs. Around her neck she'd slung at least two dozen thick brassy chains, which fell to around her navel, and clunked as she danced around singing lewdly about maracas.

One chain carried her name in chunky letters:

BARBARA. Presumably in case she got so drunk that she forgot it.

A bit later on she opened her suitcase to show Mum some of her new purchases for the holiday. First, she fished out a bikini that looked as though it had been made from no more than five thin strings loosely tied together, then she extracted a pair of see-through knickers which she waved around whilst cackling something about what a good time some lucky Spanish waiter was going to have. Gross!

Didn't think there was anyone who could make Mum look classy right now but Barbara has managed the seemingly impossible.

Dad got back a bit early to drive them to the airport. Managed to corner him in the kitchen first and hissed to him that I didn't think he should let Mum go and that Barbara was a bad influence. Talk about role reversal!

However, Dad said that Mum was determined to make an eejit of herself abroad as well as at home and wouldn't be satisfied until she'd done so. He hoped that maybe when she'd made a complete arse of herself in Spain she'd come to her senses and settle back down.

Not much hope of that if you ask me but nobody ever does.

SaTURDaY JULY 1ST

Dull rainy day so spent the afternoon online chatting to Liz, Julian, Chris and Ian.

Dad came in to see what I was doing and to use the computer. He said, 'Bloody hell, Kelly Ann, I thought you were supposed to be good at English. Don't they teach any grammar or spelling any more at your school?'

Poor Dad. He just doesn't understand online chat. He only learned to send emails a couple of months ago and still writes stuff like 'Dear John' and 'yours sincerely'.

Signed off with my usual, 'Gotta go coz dads here. c u.'

SUNDaY JULY 2ND

Didn't think it was possible for MNP to get any more uninteresting, but she has. All she can think about is pregnancy and babies. She's started knitting little cardigans for God's sake. What self-respecting newborn is going to want to wear a sad woollen cardigan?

At least she's stopped being sick and no longer eats porridge and beetroot exclusively. She's added puréed banana and raw onion sandwiches to her diet. Great.

TUESDAY JULY 4TH

Stephanie is going to Turkey on Friday with her dad and his girlfriend Danielle but Julian has decided not to interrupt his therapy sessions at such a delicate time and will be staying home. Saw Danielle this afternoon when she and her dad gave Stephanie and me a lift into town. Stephanie's dad is short, stout and balding. His French girlfriend Danielle is petite, blonde, beautiful, and looks about twenty. As we drove to Argyle Street in his new BMW, Danielle anxiously toyed with the sapphire and diamond earrings he had given her as a holiday present and constantly asked him to check the time on his Rolex watch.

I remember enquiring afterwards – no offence of course – what on earth Danielle saw in him.

Stephanie just said that I had a lot to learn. Stephanie can be extremely irritating at times.

WEDNESDAY JULY 5TH

Was surprised to see MnP reading a book tonight as lately the most intellectually challenging activity she's tried is scanning Mothercare catalogues to compare cots and potty designs. Maybe she's not brain-dead after all but has just been in a vegetative state.

When she put the book down and left the room, I just had to check out what had lured her out of cabbage country.

The title wasn't promising: *Your Pregnancy*. The contents page had riveting stuff like, 'Your Pregnancy, the Three Trimesters', 'Your Pregnancy, Month by Month', 'Your Pregnancy, Day by Day'.

So I spoke too soon. She's still in nursery la-la-land.

THURSDAY JULY 6TH

Chris came round to see me before he goes on holiday to Spain tomorrow.

Went for a saunter in the park as it was quite warm and sunny. Saw Ms Conner walking her dog and bizarrely it was male. Even stranger, she seemed really fond of it, as every now and then she would stop and scratch its ears and let it lick her face. Yuk.

Still, it's good to know that her dislike of males is confined to humans.

Saw some beautiful pink tulips and remarked on how much I liked them to Chris so he plucked one and presented it to me with a flourish, saying something daft about how it wasn't nearly as beautiful as me.

Unfortunately an old park worker saw us and started ranting on about us being vandals, and how he was sick of this yob culture, and why don't they bring back the birch and hanging, and that would soon teach us.

Thought it was a bit OTT for picking one flower, myself. Sounded like if he got his way he'd have cut off our heads and impaled them on the fence as a warning to the rest.

Just then Ms Conner caught up with us and decided to come to our defence.

She informed the park worker that this was common ground belonging to the entire community and it was not for him to dictate how it was to be used.

She told him that every citizen, including the youth of today, had rights and that these rights were not to be infringed by anyone, including police and militia, never mind frustrated pseudo-authority figures like him.

She said she would be prepared to defend these same rights even if it meant taking our case through the courts to the highest judiciary in the land and invoking the Human Rights Act.

Then she added that referring to her fine students as vandals and yobs was a slanderous affront that could not be tolerated. She ranted on some more in the same vein, by which time I was beginning to feel a bit sorry for the man, but there's no stopping Ms Conner when, well, when she doesn't feel like stopping.

Afterwards walked back home with Chris. He told me he would send me a postcard and should take care of myself, then said, 'Bye then.'

I said, 'OK, see ya.'

FRIDAY JULY 7TH

Mum, Stephanie and Chris are all out of the country now. Dad is working all the time, MNP is engrossed with her foetus and Liz is all wrapped up in Julian. It's going to be a long summer.

SUNDAY JULY 9TH

Haven't seen G in so long. Thought about going round to his place and hanging around outside in the hope of bumping into him but that seemed too much like stalking even to me and Liz has threatened to have me sectioned if I try it.

MONDAY JULY 10TH

Got an email from Stephanie. She said that she was having a fab time but didn't see much of her dad and Danielle as they spent most of the time 'resting' in bed, apparently recovering from jet lag. Stephanie said the locals were friendly. Everywhere she went some Turkish blokes would follow about a centimetre behind her; near enough for her to feel their hot breath on her neck, and sometimes their erections on her back.

Stephanie said she'd learned a useful Turkish phrase which roughly translated meant, 'I have syphilis right now. Please come back when my infection has cleared up.' She said they would then usually melt away faster than snow in the desert. Then she said she had to go as she was going paragliding with a totally fit Turkish instructor. She says the lessons cost fifty pounds a go and she's on her sixth lesson but she has persuaded her dad of her enthusiasm for her new-found hobby and anyway she has to have something to do whilst he and Danielle are 'resting'.

TUESDAY JULY 11TH

Thought I needed some exercise so went for a long walk which just happened to take me past G's place but there was no sign of him.

WEDNESDAY JULY 12TH

Under questioning confessed to Liz who has, as predicted, threatened to have me committed but settled for a promise not to come within five hundred metres of G's place again unless invited (some chance) or having her restraining order rescinded.

THURSDAY JULY 13TH

Got a postcard from Chris. He said he's having a great time but missing me. Was a bit surprised to realize I was missing him too.

FRIDAY JULY 14TH

Stephanie is back. She said she'd had a great time but that her dad had got sunburned on his bum (apparently whilst getting amorous with Danielle on a deserted island) so they had to stay another day as he couldn't face the long flight back in his condition.

SATURDAY JULY 15TH

Mum is still on holiday. She phoned Dad to say that she

and Barbara had a deal going where they could stay an extra week for a tenner. Told Dad he should insist Mum come home but as usual he paid no attention.

SUNDaY JULY 16TH

Met up with Liz and we went to see Stephanie and Julian, who are leaving for a short holiday in Tenerife with their mum. Was surprised to find that Stephanie had packed just one small carry-on bag as she usually travels with enough luggage to sink the *Titanic*. On inspection, it contained a bottle of sun cream, six thongs and a sarong. She says that's all anyone wears there.

Liz looked a bit annoyed at that but Julian reassured her by getting all soppy and telling her how much he was going to miss her. He even talked about cancelling the trip at one point but then Liz couldn't resist launching into some spiel about coping with separation anxiety and avoidance of co-dependence in relationships etc. They went off to Julian's room for further discussion (yeah right) and a spot of emergency therapy.

I don't fancy Julian at all but can't help feeling jealous that Liz has someone who really likes her and will miss her. Wish there was someone who felt that way about me.

MONDAY JULY 17TH

Chris is back. He phoned and suggested we meet up for pizza. He looked very tanned and fit so was getting a lot of attention from the girls in the restaurant, especially from the waitress who was serving us. She was really pretty so I offered to make it plain to her that we weren't a couple (have become resigned to people's daft ideas) but Chris said he wasn't interested and said not to bother. Was quite glad really as enough of my friends are paired up already.

TUESDAY JULY 18TH

Got a postcard from Mum. It said: 'Having a fantastic time, glad you're not here. Ha ha! Weather fantastic. How's the rain at home? Luv, Señora Moira.'

WEDNESDAY JULY 19TH

Bloody raining again. Some summer.

Dad is a lousy cook too. He does make a good sausage sandwich and I can manage a passable scrambled egg on toast but that's about it. We've no money for takeaways, except for the odd bag of chips, and I'm getting fed up with those. It doesn't affect MNP, of course, as she currently only eats Crunchie bars with grapefruit juice (mixed to a smooth paste with a blender). Yuk.

Never mind, Mum should be home tomorrow. Hurrah!

THURSDAY JULY 20TH

Mum is not coming home. She phoned Aunt Kate to say she will be staying in Spain to 'find herself' and to tell my dad.

FRIDAY JULY 21ST

Dad met Mum's awful travelling pal Barbara at the airport. She said what Mum has found is a 22-year-old Spanish waiter called Sergio.

SUNDAY JULY 23RD

Found Barbara's number and called her. She says it's true. When I asked her why Mum had done this, she cackled something about 'washboard abs and hung like a donkey'.

Slammed the phone down.

TUESDAY JULY 25TH

Dad is going to Spain today to get Mum back. Maybe he is going to fight Sergio for her, like a duel or something. Wonder if that's legal there?

Phoned Liz and told her what was going on but made her promise not to tell anyone else. Liz says I can rely on her professional confidentiality. She says psychologists are like Catholic priests and can never divulge secrets to another living soul, even under threat of prosecution, torture, or death.

Told her to can it but to come over anyway. Liz arrived ten minutes later and I asked her about the Spanish legal situation with regards to duels and the like. Liz said she wasn't sure, but she believed that duels are probably outlawed now. However, she thought that maybe they have the same kind of crime of passion thing like France, so that Dad can kill Sergio if he likes, as long as it's a spur of the moment thing. Ideally, he should shoot Sergio while he's doing it with my mum. Chances are he'd get off scot free or he might get garrotted, she wasn't sure.

Cut Liz off then. Just didn't want to think about that. The thought of Mum doing it with anyone, never mind a Spanish waiter, was just too gross.

Aunt Kate came to stay over and started spring-cleaning the house from top to bottom. Couldn't see the point of that but Liz said she was probably trying to impose physical order on the house to compensate for the emotionally messy uncertainty of our current family situation.

Aunt Kate told her that if she wanted to help she should stop talking rubbish and dust the living room.

She also made a huge pot of stew, an enormous dish of lasagne, and around two dozen fruit scones. She told Liz the cooking was a vain attempt to compensate for inner emptiness and the existential meaninglessness of life but asked her if she'd like a scone anyway.

Liz said, 'Two, thanks.'

WEDNESDAY JULY 26TH

No news from Dad.

THURSDAY JULY 27TH

Still no news from Dad.

FRIDAY JULY 28TH

Dad has been arrested. Brilliant. Now my mum's an adulterous slapper and my dad's a criminal. Maybe I could just pretend to everyone that they've both died in a tragic accident abroad.

Tried to talk to MNP about how we should handle things but she just said it was too bad our mum and dad couldn't behave more responsibly given that they were soon to be grandparents, and went back to reading 'Your Pregnancy, the Second Trimester'.

SATURDAY JULY 29TH

Aunt Kate told me that Dad had been arrested for the Spanish equivalent of breach of the peace, causing an affray or whatever.

Apparently Dad had a bit of go at Sergio outside the restaurant where he worked, swinging a punch at him and missing. Mum was furious and started hitting Dad with her high heels so someone called the police. Sergio tried to stop Mum hitting Dad so she started laying into him too. By the time the police came Mum looked to be the troublemaker but they seemed to find the situation amusing and just stood there laughing.

This annoyed my dad (he was pretty drunk) so he asked them who they thought they were laughing at and told them he'd make them laugh on the 'other sides of their faces all right'. The Spaniards, although they spoke English quite well, were mystified by this threat – no wonder, I've never quite figured it out myself – and invited him to explain further down at the local police station. Dad declined the invitation, saying, 'Away ye go, ye daft eejits,' whereupon he was arrested.

Aunt Kate said that Mum and Sergio had gone down to the police station the next day and got Dad out. He was let off with just a caution. He would be coming home tomorrow.

Minus Mum.

Aunt Kate went home tonight. She advised me and my sister just to say Mum had gone abroad to find work and leave it at that. There would be gossip, of course, but we should just to stick to our story and people would soon let up.

SUNDAY JULY 30TH

Dad came home tonight. A nice man he'd met on the flight took him in a taxi to our house and delivered him to the door. Dad was completely plastered.

He collapsed on the sofa and started snoring immediately so I took off his shoes and covered him with a blanket. Poor Dad.

Just as well the Good Samaritan fellow passenger had looked after him. Pity he left without giving us his name or address as I would have liked to send a note of thanks.

MONDAY JULY 31ST

The Good Samaritan was a local reporter.

The headlines read: GLASGOW'S REAL-LIFE SHIRLEY VALENTINE and then it got worse. There was: 'Heartbroken husband's desperate last-ditch flight to get wife back fails as his love is spurned in favour of more sun, sea, sangria and sex.' This was followed by details of names, addresses and so on, as well as a brief family history, then more about Mum and her 'lusty Lothario'.

So much for keeping it quiet. Now the whole world knows for sure that at least one of my parents still has sex. It's totally gross.

TUESDAY AUGUST 1ST

Stephanie's back. Of course she's heard all. She's coming round tonight with Liz to discuss tactics, whatever that means.

Dad has sobered up and got over his hangover. He looked pretty shamefaced and just mumbled, 'Sorry, love,' but he didn't go to work this morning and I think he's off to the pub this afternoon.

Got a surprise phone call of support from Ms Conner. She said she was appalled by the article in the local paper and that it represented the worst of the gutter press. She said that not only was it intrusive and prurient, but that it was also extremely poorly written. She intended to compose a strongly worded letter of complaint to the editor, enclosing an amended and improved version of the piece which she would insist on being published along with a note of apology.

Tried to dissuade her as I thought it might just

make things worse but she wouldn't hear of it.

Stephanie marched in tonight, ready for action.

First, she warned me that I'd be getting a lot of attention from boys for a while. I wish. According to her, they'd be slavering round me like hounds at the hunt. As my sister is preggers and my mum's having an affair they'll be hoping, she says, that a bit of wantonness runs in the family. She says I have to make the most of the opportunities coming my way and don't go for any dross.

Secondly, she said that we have to find Dad a girl-friend straight away, make sure Mum finds out about it and then Mum will be back home faster than a bounced cheque.

Stephanie brushed aside my doubts. The relationship with Sergio wouldn't last. No woman, she assured me, could stand the thought of her ex being happy or, perish the thought, happier with a new woman. It would work.

Stephanie also rubbished Liz's cautions about grieving periods and self-esteem exercises for Dad. 'We don't have time for all that psychobabble now. Let's check out his wardrobe for pulling clothes.'

Stephanie's confidence wavered a bit as she inspected Dad's wardrobe. She removed jackets, trousers and shirts from hangers then tossed them aside in a crumpled heap on the floor after the briefest of assessments. She opened his sock and underwear drawer and quickly closed it again, muttering something about how an emergency shopping trip was needed.

By the time she'd finished only a pair of blue jeans and a white T-shirt remained (so James Dean) plus an old-fashioned vest (turns some women on).

Stephanie admitted that her project might be a little more difficult than she first thought but she wasn't seriously discouraged until Dad returned a bit later.

We heard him before we saw him. He was singing a loud, impassioned rendition of 'Delilah' (oh God, as if we needed any more attention from our neighbours). I quickly opened the door and spotted him swaying along the street still holding a can of beer and singing loudly.

Rushed out and ushered him into the house. He stopped singing long enough to slur 'Hello grills' at Stephanie and Liz before staggering up the stairs to the bathroom, still singing, but pausing occasionally to belch.

Stephanie said that maybe Liz was right and Dad needed some time to grieve.

WEDNESDAY AUGUST 2ND

Guess what? G called me. Wonder how he got my number? Never mind. Anyway, guess what?! He said maybe we should get together sometime!!!

I can't believe it. He said he'd heard about my mum leaving for that Spanish guy and that maybe I needed someone to comfort me! Oh my God. Imagine. G wants to comfort me.

Unfortunately, he was leaving for his holiday in Egypt in an hour but he said that if I was all alone, and I needed a half hour or so of comforting, he'd come right over.

Told him that I wasn't alone, that my aunt Kate and my dad were both here but to come over anyway but he said no, that he didn't want to intrude on my family at such a delicate time. G is so thoughtful! Anyway, maybe it's best he didn't come over right away as I have two spots on my chin and need to wash my hair. This way I'll have time to prepare myself for his return in a fortnight.

Can't wait! I feel I can cope with anything now. Runaway mothers, drunken dads, pregnancy-obsessed sisters – nothing can worry me now. Am just so happy I could explode.

THURSDAY AUGUST 3RD

Not a good day. Stephanie and Liz tried to pour cold water on my news about G, questioning his motives. Honestly, they seem to have some sort of blind spot when it comes to him, and I told them so, but Liz just snorted, saying that was a laugh, *me* talking about blind spots.

Saw Chris later while browsing in WH Smith's and was going to stop for a chat but he just muttered, 'Hi,

Kelly Ann,' and moved off. He seemed embarrassed. Maybe he doesn't want to be seen with me now that our family's name has been trashed in the papers. Must say I felt quite hurt. Well, very hurt actually. Didn't think Chris would ever let me down. Didn't think it would matter so much to me either. But it does somehow.

FRIDAY AUGUST 4TH

Julian has been given his very last, final ultimatum. He's to find a job by the end of the week or start working for his dad's portable toilet business.

Liz and I met at Stephanie's for an emergency consultation. Julian looked really depressed. Seems his dad's dead serious this time and has his mum's backing, so that's that. It isn't really the portable toilet business as such, more the thought of working for his dad that's getting him down.

Liz supports him. She says it's vital that he establish his autonomous, individual identity and prevent Oedipal rivalry by finding gainful employment outside the familial environment.

Stephanie says working for his dad's mobile bog shop would drive Julian more stark raving bonkers than he already is, so I guess that she agrees with Liz.

Spent the first part of the evening seriously scouring newspapers and searching the Internet for jobs without success. However, after Julian smuggled a couple of bottles of wine up from the kitchen, we seemed to find inspiration and soon Stephanie spotted the perfect position for him.

A local company called Hunky House Husbands Ltd is looking for staff. Applicants have to be attractive, outgoing young males. An aptitude for housework was desirable but not essential. All Julian would have to do is a little light housework whilst wearing almost no clothes and wealthy older women would pay twenty pounds an hour. Seemed ideal.

The advert specified that CVs must be accompanied by full-length photos of applicants so Stephanie got out her camera while Julian went off to 'slip into something more comfortable'.

Didn't like to say but I thought that maybe Julian would be considered too skinny to qualify as a 'hunk'. However, when he came back waving a feather duster and wearing just a bow tie and a thong, I could see that he had certain attributes that more than made up for his lack of bulky muscle. Julian was massively endowed and then some. Glanced at Liz. She had a sly gleam in her eye that told me this wasn't exactly a new revelation to her. Therapy sessions my arse!

SATURDAY AUGUST 5TH

Liz is seeing Julian tonight and Stephanie has a date with Dave so I suppose I'll just have to spend the night watching telly. Would normally ring Chris but not after the way he froze me out.

Wonder if G will call me when he gets back from holiday? What if he meets some gorgeous blonde and falls madly in love with her? Probably her family will totally approve of him and welcome him with open arms as their future son-in-law. If they're wealthy, they'll probably offer to send him to the same college as their daughter, and then provide the couple with a fabulous house in Egypt so that he never comes home and I won't get to see him ever again.

SUNDAY AUGUST 6TH

So worried and depressed about the prospect of G meeting someone on holiday that I resorted to mentioning my concerns to Stephanie. She was pretty sarcastic as usual but her reply did cheer me up as she made the following points.

1. Blonde Egyptian girls are about as rare as three-humped camels.
2. No self-respecting Egyptian father would allow G

within a hundred metres of his (blonde or otherwise) daughter.

3. In the unlikely event that G did somehow manage to form a relationship with a young Egyptian girl, he would be cut into tiny pieces by her family and fed to the village goats.

Feel so much better.

MONDaY AUGUST 7TH

Awful day. Got about twenty text messages from stupid first and second years asking for a date as they'd heard I was into younger guys like my mum.

Am so humiliated and have spent most of the day sobbing. Just wish I were dead. Can't ever go back to school, that's for sure, so will just have to run off to London and live on the streets, foraging through bins for my dinner and begging for coins outside tube stations with a HOMELESS AND HUNGARY sign written in deliberately bad English slung round my neck. Probably, I'll end up having to become a prostitute and eventually will be strangled by a weird client.

Bet Mum will be sorry then. She'll fly back for my funeral, and fling herself over my coffin, weeping inconsolably. People will try to drag her off but she'll cling on desperately, crying that it's all her fault but now it's too late. Afterwards, of course, she'll give up Sergio, become a nun, and spend the rest of her life doing good works but she'll never be able to wipe out the awful guilt.

Was interrupted in these musings by the doorbell ringing. Checked my reflection in the hall mirror before answering. Had cried so much my face was all puffy and my eyes were wee and red. In fact, I looked a lot like a pig. Don't think a career as a prostitute is an option anyway. Went to the bathroom and splashed my face with cold water before answering the door. If it was one of those first or second years I was going to kill them. But it was just Chris.

He asked how I was then said, never mind, he could see for himself. We went for a Coke and Chris explained that he hadn't been snubbing me before. He just hadn't wanted to put any pressure on me to talk about my family troubles until I was ready. He was sorry if I'd got the wrong impression and that I should know by now that he'd always be there for me if I needed him.

Chris is a great guy. Am so glad we are pals again.

TUESDAY AUGUST 8TH

Maybe Liz is wrong and there is a God after all. What a fantastic day! Started off brilliant with guess what? A postcard from G!

There was a photo of the pyramids on the front (so

romantic) and a note, not just a signature, on the back telling me that he missed me and was looking forward to seeing me when he got home. Hurrah!

But the very best news was still to come. Stephanie just called and asked me if I'd heard about Shelly Fitzgerald? Neither of us can stand Shelly. She is blonde and very pretty but that's not the only reason we don't like her. She's a stuck-up bitch who's called Stephanie a slut, told Liz she should go on a diet, and once referred to me as pizza face when I had a bad attack of spots. Since Stephanie was sounding pleased I guessed the news was bad for Shelly but was gobsmacked when she told me the details.

According to Stephanie, our family is no longer the talk of the place because, joy of joys, Shelly Fitzgerald's mum has dumped her dad and – get this – has moved in with the school janitor. What's more, this very day her snooty sister appeared topless in the *Sun*!

Can hardly believe my luck. This scandal surely knocks ours into second place. Thank you, God!

FRIDAY AUGUST 11TH

Went round to Stephanie's with Liz. Julian was there and so I took the opportunity to ask him how his job as a hunky house husband was going.

At first he refused to discuss it but Liz and I pressed

him and Stephanie threatened to tell all anyway, so he eventually agreed with only token resistance.

Apparently his first client turned out to be an old friend of his mum's called Claire who used to babysit him and Stephanie when they were little. Nevertheless she wasn't put off and just kept remarking how big he'd grown and, according to Julian, she wasn't looking at his face when she said it.

However, when he offered to dust the lounge, she declined, saying she remembered the Wedgwood bowl and Edinburgh crystal vase he'd broken on his last visit to her house (Julian used to be a bit clumsy it seems).

Anyway, eventually the woman settled on Julian doing a spot of ironing for her (it would keep him stationary and so hopefully avoid mishaps) while she put her feet up and watched.

Unfortunately, Julian had never done any ironing before and pressed her pure silk blouse using the linen setting, thereby not only failing to eliminate any creases – he didn't unfold and spread the garment first – but also leaving a large brown iron mark down the front.

However, Claire hadn't seemed too upset, merely telling him that his services would no longer be required and even slipping him a fiver as a tip, muttering something about at least the visit hadn't cost her too much, just seventy pounds or so – not in the same league as his previous stay at her home (setting her back hundreds) – and to tell his mum she was asking about her.

Nevertheless Julian declared himself demoralized and in need of therapy for unresolved self-esteem issues so Liz and he went off to his bedroom for a spot of 'counselling'.

SATURDAY AUGUST 12TH

Horrors! Have just realized that our exam results are due on Tuesday. How could I have forgotten such a thing given that my entire future will be determined by this single event?

Am sick with worry as all I can remember is the mistakes I've made. Oh if only I'd written πr^2 instead of πr and not referred to Nelson Mandela as Horatio Nelson in my essay on political reform in South Africa.

Phoned Liz and Stephanie but they were both out with their boyfriends so texted Chris who came over after football practice with a packet of Jaffa Cakes, a bottle of Irn Bru, and a horror video. He was quite sweet, telling me not to worry and that he was sure I'd be OK and feeding me Jaffa Cakes like tranquillizers.

The movie was great and really helped take my mind off the exam results as it was about vampires, which I've always found kind of sexy as well as scary. How weird is that?

Afterwards, I made tea and toast and we just chatted for a while. Chris kept pouncing on me from behind and pretending to bite my jugular whenever my conversation strayed to exam results so that helped keep me off the subject.

He was just about to get ready to leave when my dad returned from the pub. Dad was totally pissed, of course, but trying to hide it by talking very slowly . . . and . . . carefully . . . with . . . exaggerated . . . politeness. The effect was spoiled somewhat when he kept calling Chris, Liz, and totally ruined when he tripped on the way upstairs to the bathroom and slid bumpily to the bottom.

Chris ran to help him but Dad shrugged him off, muttering something about 'must get that middle step fixed', and managed to get up and make his way back upstairs swaying only slightly.

Would have been mortified by the whole episode if it had been witnessed by anyone else but it was only Chris so didn't feel too bad. Don't know what I'll do if I start going out with G. Won't be able to bring him to the house without first locking up Dad in the attic like Mr Rochester's mad wife in *Jane Eyre*.

Imagine me going out with G! Can't wait until he gets back from holiday. How could I have worried about exams when I'm to become G's girlfriend? Am so happy I could burst.

SUNDAY AUGUST 13TH

Maybe G would not want a bimbo failure for girlfriend. Oh God, hope I do OK. Feel really nervous again.

Must admit I wish Mum were here. I know what she'd say of course: that I could only do my best and that's all anyone could ask for, and anyway, what's done was done and there was no point in crying over spilt milk, and besides, she was sure I'd do fine and would I find the TV remote control so that she could see if *EastEnders* had started and bring her fags over.

Really miss Mum sometimes, even her lousy clichés and annoying habits of losing the TV remote control and smoking. Wish she hadn't done this.

MONDay AUGUST 14TH

Got a postcard from Mum. It said she knew that my exam results were due soon and that I wasn't to worry, that I could only do my best and that's all anyone could ask for, and that anyway what's done is done and there was no point in crying over spilt milk, and besides, she was sure I'd do fine.

She also said that she hoped I'd understand one day why she'd had to leave to 'find herself' and that it wasn't easy for her either and that she really missed *EastEnders*.

Stephanie rang. She says she's heard that all the results are going to be late and that they were all wrong anyway so it didn't matter that much that they were going to be late in any case.

Honestly, how could Stephanie believe this ridiculous sensationalist rumour? Didn't think she was as gullible as all that. Of course a large professional exam body couldn't possibly make a major balls-up like that. Not with something that affects the future of so many people. The exam results were far too important to mess up. The educational establishment, the government and everybody wouldn't allow that to happen. It was just ridiculous.

TUESDAY AUGUST 15TH

Got up at five o'clock in the morning as couldn't sleep and also wanted to make sure I didn't miss the post.

Mail came at ten o'clock but no exam results, just a letter from *Reader's Digest* telling Dad he might be the lucky winner of £250,000. Or maybe not.

WEDNESDAY AUGUST 16TH

Still no exam results.

FRIDAY AUGUST 18TH

At last results arrived. Just stared at the large envelope for a while as though it were an unexploded bomb before taking a deep breath to steady myself and tearing it open with trembling hands.

Spent the next half hour trying to figure out what the hell it all meant as bits and pieces of partial results were all over the place. Thought of ringing someone up to ask how to make sense of the stuff but was afraid I might sound stupid.

Finally managed to decipher contents . . . I think.

Was gutted to have failed English, which I'd hoped to do well in, but was delighted to have got a high grade in history, which I was sure I'd made a mess of, and gobsmacked to have obtained a grade one (the highest possible) in German, especially as I'd never done the course, let alone sat the exam. Hmmm . . .

Called Stephanie but she hadn't bothered to check her mail yet as she was too busy but said she'd probably take a look tomorrow if she could find the time.

Phoned Liz. Like me, she was still trying to figure out what it all meant but was sure she'd passed something – she just wasn't sure what.

Chris hadn't received any results, just a letter saying that whilst they had a note of his candidate number they hadn't been able to match it to any exam scripts and was he sure he actually was who he said he was.

As the day wore on I heard more odd results. Mohammed Abdullah Rashid was puzzled to have done so well in Hebrew Studies and Gaelic (neither of which he could remember attempting but, well, as Abdullah philosophically accepted, two passes are better than the one in Arabic he'd been expecting), whilst the Chaikovsky twins were furious at having got the bottom grade for their Russian Higher and wrote a letter of complaint to the exam authorities in perfect Russian (except for a few colourful and unflattering colloquialisms roughly translated as 'this examination authority has the brains of a chicken's backside').

Jennifer Tully's granny would have been pleased at passing her Higher maths although the certificate will have to be awarded posthumously as she died ten years ago.

Against the advice of Stephanie (treat 'em mean, keep 'em keen) and Liz (who cares how that tosser has done), I phoned G to see how he'd got on but the family must still be on holiday as I got no answer either from his mobile or the house phone. Left a message to say I hoped he'd enjoyed his holiday and had done well in the Standard Grades and that he could phone me when he got back if he liked.

SATURDAY AUGUST 19TH

What do exams matter anyway? How could I have got my priorities so wrong? G texted to say he'd just got back but was so knackered he intended to sleep through the weekend. Poor thing. Then he said he'd see me Monday at school!

Just two days more! Am so excited I can hardly wait. Oh, G, how I've missed you! Soon, we'll be together for ever.

MONDay AUGUST 21ST

Got up at five am to prepare. Had a bath and exfoliated, cleansed and moisturized whole body. Washed hair with Clean and Clarify shampoo to remove build-up of hair-care products, then applied volumizing conditioner, Sleek and Smooth moisturizing gel, Sheer Gloss finishing rinse, No Frizz straightener mousse and heat-activated Protect and Detangle spray, before blow drying each individual hair to silky perfection.

Only thing was that it looked a bit greasy when finished so had to remove all the haircare products with Clean and Clarify again before repeating the whole process, this time with the addition of Lemon Oil Reduction Miracle Mask between the Sleek and Smooth moisturizing gel and the Sheer Gloss finishing rinse.

My arms ached after the second blow-drying and not for the first time I cursed God for giving me curly hair. Still, at last it looked pretty good.

Next, I applied extract of sea algae face mask, which promised a glowing, perfect complexion by flushing out toxins and refreshing dull skin with the invigorating power of natural marine products.

Looked pretty daft with my face covered in bright blue-green paste, and supposed I looked even more stupid with the slices of cucumber I put over my eyes, but of course couldn't see myself after that. However, was confident it would be worth it to obtain a perfect complexion.

After half an hour the mask had dried and it was time to take it off. However, as it was still only ten past seven, decided to give it another half hour so that the mask could work even better.

Unfortunately I fell asleep. When I woke it was already eight o'clock so ran to bathroom to rinse the mask off. Succeeded only in changing light blue chalky consistency to deep green gloopy gunge but could not scrub it off.

Was running short of time so decided to remove the showerhead from stand to power blast my face. This did remove the mask but unfortunately had the effect of forcing half of it up my nose with the remainder lodged in various blobs and streaks in my hair . . . so hair wash routine again but no time to blow-dry.

Eventually removed most of mask from hair and body. It was now nearly nine o'clock so was going to be late for sure when I discovered that I did not have a clean pair of knickers.

Briefly considered spraying yesterday's pair with perfume and chancing it but decided I'd better quickly wash them (just in case). Had to put them on still wet and hope that body heat would dry them out before I developed thrush.

Managed to get to school before the start of fifth year assembly but not before Miss McElwee spotted me and told me this was a poor start to the school year and asked me why I had a damp patch on my skirt and green nostrils.

Couldn't see G at the assembly despite craning my neck to scan the entire hall and briefly standing up on my seat. Was told off for this by Miss McElwee – she seems to really have it in for me – and she didn't seem to believe my explanation that I was just trying to get a better view of Mr Smith as he was delivering his beginning of term address to us (especially, I suppose, since I was facing in the opposite direction to the podium and searching the back rows at the time).

Anyway, Mr Smith told us not to worry too much about the Standard Grade results as these were mostly irrelevant to colleges and universities. The only things that really matter to us fifth years going on to higher education were our Higher exams and so our whole future depends on how we do in these this year. Huh, so now they tell us – so much for all the work and worry last year then.

G didn't turn up all day. Despite Liz and Stephanie's advice, I called to see what was up. G's mum answered, saying that he was in the toilet with the runs, and if only he'd listened to her about not drinking the tap water he wouldn't have had this problem. She added that G would probably be back at school tomorrow as this was no doubt a twenty-four-hour thing.

TUESDAY AUGUST 22ND

Beauty routine went more smoothly this time and was finished by eight. Since it was too early to go to school I just decided to lie down on the couch and relax for ten minutes. Unfortunately fell asleep and was late again. G has still not returned to school. Can't face getting G's mum on the phone again so have to get up early tomorrow to prepare just in case G has recovered.

WEDNESDAY AUGUST 23RD

Didn't wake until nearly six this morning but fortunately was able to complete beauty routine and would have been on time if I hadn't knocked over an open can of beer Dad had left on the kitchen table last night. Had to spend fifteen minutes trying to blot the stuff off my skirt and mop the floor at the same time. Now have detention with Mr Smith on Thursday for persistent late coming and have been referred to Guidance for counselling because of possible alcohol abuse problem.

Can't stand my guidance teacher. She's supposed to listen to me and look after my 'personal and social welfare' but she's just plain nosy if you ask me and will probably question me endlessly over this. Great!

G did not turn up today again and no one has commented on how different I look (except for Chris, who said I seemed a bit tired and was I OK? Thanks a bunch, Chris) so am beginning to wonder if beauty routine is worth it. Maybe I'll leave out the cucumber treatment as they seem to be giving me dark circles under my eyes.

Guess what? G finally rang to say he wouldn't be at school tomorrow as he still has the runs. Disappointed that I won't be seeing G tomorrow. Must admit, though, it will be good to give the beauty routine a miss and get some sleep at last.

THURSDaY AUGUST 24TH

Bollocks! Woke at four am anyway as am now used to getting up at that time. Tossed and turned for ages before finally falling asleep sometime after seven. Next thing I knew it was half past nine and I was late again.

Then, guess what? G was at school after all. I spotted him at break time as he was heading for the football pitch. At first I tried to hide behind the large playground bins as I so wanted our first meeting after the holidays to be special and I knew I looked a state with my hair all frizzy, my skirt unironed and a large spot developing just under my nose. However, he saw me and sauntered over. He asked what I was doing rummaging around behind the bins then remarked on how tired I looked and what was I up to at night that meant I wasn't getting enough sleep he'd like to know.

It wasn't really the reunion I'd dreamed of but at least he'd noticed me and even smiled his gorgeous cute smile at me, so I tried to look poised and kind of mysterious which was quite difficult under the circumstances, and said, wouldn't he just like to know, and he said, yes, he really would like to hear all about it and why didn't I meet him after school by the bus stop?

Was so excited I could hardly speak but just about managed to croak 'Yes, please,' before Liz came up and asked what on earth I was doing standing beside all that rubbish and she wasn't talking about the contents of the bins either.

Honestly, I don't expect Liz to be able to appreciate someone of G's depth and class but she could try to be a bit less bloody rude. Still, was too ecstatic to be really annoyed. G wanted to see me, just me, and actually asked me specially. Spent the rest of the afternoon in a cloud of absolute happiness, grinning inanely at everyone, even Mr Smith, who stopped me just as I was about to leave for the bus stop and my appointment with G.

Stopped grinning when he reminded me that I had detention with him and where did I think I was going?

Begged him to postpone my detention until tomorrow but he refused. Offered to attend detention all of next week instead but he still refused and told me not to try his patience. Finally agreed to report for detention for the rest of my entire life, even after I'd left school, if he'd only just on this single occasion let me go and that my entire future happiness depended on it.

Mr Smith said that he was sorry that my entire future happiness depended on it but that pupils' happiness or otherwise was not his concern, only their punctuality, and marched me off to detention.

Phoned G the moment I got home and explained the situation, telling him how devastated I was and that I'd never forgive Smith as long as he lived and that I'd hate him (Smith) to my dying day.

G said it was cool and he hadn't waited long anyway. He agreed, however, that Smith was a tosser and then said maybe he would see me tomorrow.

FRIDAY AUGUST 25TH

Saw G at school today and he said he'd call me. Am so excited.

1:30 am

Suppose I should really put this under tomorrow's date but it still feels like tonight. Had thought that G meant he would call me tonight but come to think of it he didn't actually say when he would call.

Liz said that on no account was I to call or text G as this would place me in a psychologically inferior position. To distract me, she insisted I go over to her place to watch a DVD about a psychotic serial killer while we tried out a new honey and lemon face pack she'd found. She said she wasn't on a diet at the moment so wouldn't put me off the movie by trying to lick the pack off.

The film did manage to distract me but unfortunately I now can't sleep for fear a crazed killer will break into my room and slaughter me slowly with a toothpick. Thanks, Liz.

SUNDaY AUGUST 27TH

No call from G so I phoned him (against Liz and Stephanie's advice of course) only to get his bloody mum again, who had picked up his mobile as he was in the shower. Was forced to chat to her for almost twenty minutes whilst all the time imagining G in the shower (mmmm . . .) before being cut off for some unknown reason.

MONDAY AUGUST 28TH

At school I found out that, apparently, the batteries on G's phone had gone flat and G had no money left in his phone to call back afterwards. He said we must get together sometime and maybe go out one night. Am so happy. Finally, I'm almost someone's girlfriend and not just anyone's girlfriend but the girlfriend of the most gorgeous guy in the school. Am so excited I could burst.

TUESDAY AUGUST 29TH

Ha ha, told you so, Stephanie and Liz! They thought G was just stringing me along and wouldn't actually name a date but he has! We're going to meet outside the Odeon at seven-thirty on Thursday to see something or other. Didn't catch what film, as I was so totally excited that I couldn't concentrate on what he was saying, but I did manage to say 'Yes, please,' and 'Thanks, that would be just terrific,' and that I 'couldn't wait'.

At last I've got a real genuine date! Finally feel like a proper teenage girl who goes out with boys. Hallelujah!!!

Begged Dad for money to buy a new outfit for date. Felt bad as I timed the request to coincide with happy carefree stage of his (now almost nightly) drinking that comes before the maudlin angry stage (typically accompanied by wailing and tuneless rendition of 'Delilah').

Took the day off to shop for a new outfit. Stephanie insisted on coming with me – she said she doesn't trust me to shop on my own and besides she'd only be missing double maths, English, biology and French.

We met outside Fraser's and Stephanie was about to march me inside with an imperious, 'This will do for a start,' when I pointed out that I couldn't afford to shop there and suggested TopShop. She demanded to know how much I was planning to spend, and then muttered something about 'mission bloody impossible'.

Two hours and ten shops later I was beginning to get a bit fed up with Stephanie's moaning. She had pissed off a lot of shop assistants with imperious demands for them to fetch this and that outfit to the changing room and couldn't they just alter this or that seam, hemline, or zipper. Anyway, finally she did pick out this outfit – sludge-green trousers with beige top which sounds minging but looked fantastic. Stephanie says the colours are this season's muted moss and dark café-crème, but whatever, they looked great on me and the whole outfit was really cheap. Well, it was really cheap until Stephanie insisted I buy a leather belt to go with it, which was more expensive than the trousers and top together. She says expensive accessories are a must with cheap clothes. If Stephanie didn't have such good taste and style, wasn't great fun, and such a fantastically loyal friend who'd do just about anything for me, I might not ask her to shop with me again.

Anyway, I did refuse to have my navel pierced and a ring fitted. Knowing my luck I'd only get an infection which would lead to blood poisoning, the gangrene spreading to my heart and killing me the night before my very first date ever.

Just as well I didn't spend any more money on my navel anyway as I now have hardly enough cash left over for the pictures.

G phoned tonight to ask if I was still on for the movies tomorrow or if I was too sick to go or something as I hadn't been at school. He is so thoughtful and considerate! Managed to reassure him that I was OK and that I'd definitely be there. Would be there if I had two broken arms and legs as well as double pneumonia but didn't say that of course! (Am not completely stupid like Stephanie and Liz think.) Just said he could count on me and yes, of course I could pay for his ticket as he was a bit short at the moment.

However, when G hung up I did start to worry about needing more cash. Hated to ask Dad for more as I know things are tight. Fortunately Chris came round to see if I was OK, my being off school and all that, and I was able to borrow a fiver from him. Didn't tell Chris it was for G of course, since he still harbours this ridiculous hostility towards him, so said it was to buy a takeaway as there was no food in the house but felt a bit guilty at this deception. Still, as Liz says, guilt is a destructive and useless emotion.

Can hardly wait for tomorrow!

THURSDAY AUGUST 31ST

Took another day off school in order to get ready for tonight. Did the whole beauty routine again and put on the new outfit then checked appearance in mirror. Not bad. However, it was only eleven am and I was beginning to wish I hadn't got ready so soon as it was still eight and a half hours until I had to meet G and I was so excited I could have burst.

Kept putting on different make-up then wiping it off again to pass the time until school had finished and Liz and Stephanie dropped by to check on me.

Liz said the outfit was great but that she wasn't sure about the yellow eye-shadow. I pointed out that the eye-shadow colour was actually 'touch of golden sunset allure' and not 'yellow' but Liz didn't seem any more convinced and Stephanie just told me to 'ditch the custard powder for God's sake'.

Stephanie produced a large toolbox of cosmetics, brushes, pallets and sponges and expertly set to work. By the time she'd finished I hardly recognized myself. I looked so sophisticated, just like a model in a glossy magazine.

Was feeling really happy until Liz asked if I'd told Chris last night about my date with G. Felt myself flushing scarlet as I remembered my deception about the loan. Liz spotted my red face and correctly guessed I was feeling guilty about something but I denied this as I didn't feel like talking about it. She seemed miffed – Liz always likes to know everything about everybody – and insisted that she could tell a guilt complex when she saw one and that she recommended full disclosure in order to obtain catharsis and eventual healing.

I told her that was rubbish and reminded her that she had said guilt was a destructive and useless emotion so I had decided not to bother with it. Should have known better than to challenge Liz on bloody psychology as she gleefully corrected me straight away. That was jealousy, not guilt, I was told. A sense of guilt was absolutely essential in a civilized society. Only psychopaths like Hitler, Hannibal Lecter and Mr Smith (who gave Liz detention for starting to eat a Mars bar in PE last week and confiscated the remainder of the Mars) don't feel any guilt.

Stephanie told Liz to can it as she needed to apply another coat of Luscious Lashes mascara. Thank God for that.

They left before Dad got back. Stephanie must have done a great job because even Dad noticed me and actually said, 'You look nice, Kelly Ann.' Was so gobsmacked I found myself telling him I was going on a date with a boy to the Odeon instead of lying and saying I was going to Liz's. He just smiled a bit sadly and said, 'That's nice, love,' before turning on the telly.

At least he didn't question me for hours like Mum would have done, wanting to know every last detail about G. It's just as well she's not here. Started to feel a bit tearful for some stupid reason.

It's six-thirty now and if I leave right away I'll probably be twenty minutes early instead of ten minutes late, like I've promised Liz and Stephanie, but I can't sit here any longer. I'm just too excited.

Fabulous, fabulous fabulous night! My first date ever and with G.

Did arrive twenty minutes early and G was ten minutes late so had to wait for half an hour in the rain but it was worth it when G arrived looking gorgeous and smiling at me. My G.

Must admit I was surprised and even a bit disappointed at first when I realized that he wasn't alone but had brought two of his pals, Johnny Wilson and Billy Bryson. However, thinking it over, I realized that it was actually a good sign that he wants his friends to meet me already. I wasn't going to be just a one-night stand but an important part of his whole life.

There were loads of people waiting to get into the movie and we only just managed to get tickets. We couldn't find four seats together but the usher found us three seats at the end of a row with one just behind it. Unfortunately, due to Johnny and Billy barging in front of me, I had to sit in the row behind. G was too tactful to criticize his friends in my presence but I'm sure he was embarrassed and annoyed by their bad manners. I tried to smile my support to G and I think somehow he was aware of it even though I was smiling at the back of his head.

The film was a kind of kung fu fighting type of story, which isn't really my kind of thing so I didn't mind going for the drinks during it.

After the movie we all went to the chippy. I was starving as I hadn't eaten since lunch but I'd no money left and I knew G didn't have any. I couldn't very well ask G's friends, who I really didn't know very well, to buy me supper so had to just say I wasn't hungry.

Johnny said, 'No wonder you're so skinny, Kelly Ann.' Charming. Then he turned to G. 'I suppose you'll be cadging from both of us as usual.'

The smell of hot, vinegary fish and chips was making me drool and watching them eat was torture. G was sharing Johnny's fish supper. Billy said, 'Sure you don't want any of mine, Kelly Ann?' Didn't feel I could go back on my earlier statement about not being hungry so declined again but nearly moaned with frustration when he tossed his remaining meal (less than half eaten) in the bin, saying he'd already had a curry before the film.

Johnny suggested going back to his place to try out his new PlayStation game and finish off the couple of bottles of cider he'd stolen from his big brother but I said no, it was getting late. Actually I was secretly hoping they would both shove off and give G and me some time alone together. No such luck. Somehow they managed to persuade G to join them, no doubt appealing to his strong sense of male loyalty. Never mind, there would be lots of other opportunities for us to get to know one another away from prying eyes.

Hadn't any money left for my bus fare so started to walk briskly home. It was dark by this time and I had reached a quiet road with no shops or houses, just disused factories, when a car slowed down alongside me. Caught a glimpse of the driver, who was a man with grey hair. Was really panicked so, looking straight ahead and picking up pace, I shouted at him to, 'Sod off, you old perve.'

The driver rolled down his window and said, 'That's nice, Kelly Ann.'

Dad!

He'd been a bit worried as it was getting late and he hasn't yet learned my mobile number, never mind how to text, so he'd driven round in the hope of finding me. Noticed with relief that he didn't smell of drink so he must have stayed sober in case I needed a lift tonight. This thought made me a bit teary and when I got home Stephanie's carefully applied Luscious Lashes mascara had run, trickling black rivulets down both my cheeks.

Dad made me a fried egg sandwich and a cup of tea. Heaven. Am so happy I could burst. And tomorrow I'll be seeing G at school. My boyfriend G.

FRIDAY SEPTEMBER 1ST

Only G wasn't there. Neither was Billy nor Johnny. Stephanie said they must have got rat arsed and were now too hungover to come to school but I was still worried, about G anyway. Phoned G but yet again his mum answered his mobile. She told me that G had a headache, was sick, had a parched mouth and kept drinking Irn Bru by the bucketload only to throw it up again five minutes later. She said that if G was over eighteen and it was therefore legal for him to drink alcohol she would have assumed he'd a hangover. As it was she'd accepted that he'd caught a nasty bug. To be on the safe side she was going to insist he rest up at home all weekend even if he felt better. She'd also told him if he caught this bug again a minimum of two weeks confined to home except for school times would be necessary for a full recovery.

G's mum isn't daft. Wish she hadn't grounded him this

weekend of all weekends though. Decided to send him a get well soon card anyway just so I could sign it 'Love, Kelly Ann' and put kisses on it. I am his girlfriend now after all, even if, due to those tossers Billy and Johnny, I haven't kissed him for real yet. Can't wait for everyone to know about me and G. Stephanie and Liz have refused to pass the word around in the hope, so they say, that I might yet be struck by a bolt of sanity and ditch him even if, they agreed, this is about as likely as a death row reprieve for a black man in Texas. Hilarious.

Had great idea of casually spilling the beans to Melanie Motormouth Whistler, thereby ensuring almost everyone in the Western hemisphere will know about it by lunch time. G and me, a couple at last.

SATURDAY SEPTEMBER 2ND

Can't wait to see G again on Monday and keep wandering about with a silly smile on my face all the time. Was in such a good mood, I even asked MNP how she was feeling. Instantly regretted it as she droned on for what seemed like hours about every little detail of her pregnancy and birth plan. Switched off less than halfway through and just nodded 'Yeah' to everything. Tuned in again to hear her thanking me for agreeing to be back-up birthing partner and asking whether I'd like to feel her abdomen. Er, no thanks and what on earth is a back-up birthing partner?

SUNDAY SEPTEMBER 3RD

One more day until I see G. Our very first day at school as official girlfriend and boyfriend. For once in my life I feel like a desirable, confident person who can achieve anything. So much so that when Dad told me Graham's parents had arranged to come over to meet us all at the end of the month 'to get to know our in-laws-to-be' and he would have to take us all out for a meal as Mum wasn't here to cook, I offered to cook instead. Dad was doubtful to begin with but I pointed out that I'd been doing home economics for four years now and a three-course dinner for six would be no bother at all. Didn't tell him that we'd only planned one theoretically and written it up for a test. Still, given I got nearly sixty percent for the test and a 'well done' comment from Miss McElwee for spelling and neatness, I reckon the practical bit can't be too hard. Dad was finally persuaded when I pointed out the money he would save if we ate at home.

Feel I am capable of anything now. Feel like I'm floating on air inside a big bubble of happiness! Oh G!

MONDAY SEPTEMBER 4TH

Worst day of my life.

Didn't see G in the morning. I think he must have been late and we don't share any classes on Monday. At lunch time was wandering round school with Liz and Stephanie scanning for G when Shelly Fitzgerald – the one whose mum is having it off with the janitor – came right up to me, jabbed a finger in my face and said what's all this she's hearing about me messing around with her boyfriend? Was too gobsmacked to reply as I'd no idea what she was on about but Stephanie said to her that no one would be doing anything with a boyfriend of Shelly's as there were, after all, hygiene issues to consider. Shelly said that was rich coming from a toffee-nosed tart like Stephanie, whereupon Liz intervened to suggest conflict resolution strategies and anger management therapy. However, she must have accidentally stepped on Shelly's toe with her new stiletto-heeled ankle boots – very slimming for ankles and calves apparently – because Shelly told Liz to get off her foot or she'd smack her fat face for her. Liz removed her foot with a sincere sounding 'sorry' but then accidentally elbowed Shelly in the ribs.

Things were starting to get a bit ugly when G came up behind me and hooked an arm around my shoulder. I snuggled into him and smiled, instantly forgetting the argument, which seemed so trivial with G's arm around me. But then my good mood vanished as G started talking about how he and I were just good mates and nothing else and wasn't that right, Kelly Ann? And that I was to tell Shelly not to be so daft and that of course I wasn't his girlfriend, just a pal like Johnny and Billy and wasn't that right, Kelly Ann? Found myself smiling and nodding, though my smile had probably turned into more like a rictus grin judging by how stiff my cheeks felt all of a sudden. Then G let go of me, moved over to Shelly, put his arms around her waist and they both walked off. I stood transfixed to the spot but still nodding and grinning like a total imbecile whilst I watched him nuzzle her ear.

My bubble of happiness had burst like, well . . . like a burst bubble.

TUESDaY SePTeMBeR 5TH

My life is over so there will be no further entries to this journal.

WeDNeSDaY SePTeMBeR 6TH

That didn't mean I was going to top myself. Anyway, for all the attention I get in this family no one would notice until my body had started to rot. No, it just means that life for me will no longer have any meaning or joy and I will just trudge out my futile existence in despair and heartache for ever.

THURSDAY SEPTEMBER 7TH

Well, just one more entry. A bottle of Sunny Delight burst in Shelly's bag today, ruining her maths textbook, her geography assignment, her English essay and her gym kit. Hurrah!! Coincidently, Liz's drink from her lunch box had gone missing.

FRIDAY SEPTEMBER 8TH

OK, just one other last entry. Today someone had pinned a note to the back of Shelly's jumper during English that said MY FACE IS AS UGLY AS A BABBOON'S BUM. No one likes Shelly very much in that class so she couldn't figure out for ages why everyone was sniggering at her. Don't think Ms Conner likes her either, because when Shelly did find out and complained, Ms Conner just commented about the use of such an imaginative simile and did we all know the difference between a simile and a metaphor?

Stephanie put her hand up to say that she did and then proceeded to illustrate her answer with examples. She pointed out that, '"Shelly's face is as ugly as a baboon's bum" is a simile, whereas "Shelly has a baboon's bum face" is a metaphor.'

By this time Shelly had turned scarlet with rage and embarrassment and her face looked even more like a baboon's bum in heat but Ms Conner just said, 'Quite correct, Stephanie.'

However, after class Ms Conner told me, Liz and Stephanie to stay behind. Then she told Stephanie that baboon had two 'b's in total not three and to work on her spelling. She said that she did not expect any repeat of today's incident or similar in the future and did we understand her? We said that we did. She also said that although Shelly was not an especially personable pupil, and in some people's eyes her misfortunes might appear to be an example of the operation of natural justice, a teacher's duty was to uphold the letter of the school law except when she chose not to and did we understand her? Almost said no to that as it did seem a bit obscure but thought better of it and just nodded.

Afterwards talked things over with Liz and Stephanie and we decided to abandon any further plans to get back at Shelly. Anyway, as I said, no matter what happened to her, she had G and I didn't and nothing could make up for that.

Saw Liz and Stephanie roll their eyes in that maddening there-she-goes-again way but all they said was, yeah, maybe Shelly was suffering enough.

It's late Friday night now and a long weekend looms ahead without G. And this is only the first of many long G-less weekends stretching on to infinity. Well maybe not infinity but for the rest of my life, which is much the same thing ... for me anyway. It's just that infinity sounds more poignant and sad and seems to express my feelings better. Perhaps I should use this personal tragedy to inspire my creativity and become a famous playwright or poet. Don't know whether G would fancy a famous poet or not, and if he did maybe my creative genius would dry up because I would be happy again instead of sad and tortured, then I'd lose him again because my talent and fame had gone. It's all very difficult. Still, at the moment I haven't got G and I'm not famous and talented so may as well try for one of them. Will start by composing a poem about my unrequited love for G.

G

Oh G, Oh G, Oh G,

Where art thou, Oh G?

Will you ever be,

With me?

G?

FRIDAY SEPTEMBER 15TH

Have decided to break my ban on entries to this journal because just have to record an amazing coincidence which is quite spooky really. This year's Young Writer of the Year competition is to focus on poetry and the subject is, guess what, 'Unrequited Love'.

Ms Conner is not that happy with the topic but says nonetheless that all fifth and six years are to enter and that winning the competition would not only be a great honour for the individual concerned but also for her – that is, the English department of the school. As an extra incentive she has promised that if we win we won't have to read any more poetry for the entire year. Loud cheers went up at that and people jostled each other to grab hold of the entry forms. For the rest of the lesson Ms Conner didn't talk about the poetry competition again but just gave a rather boring lecture on the use of irony in English literature and our homework was to think of examples of irony in everyday life. Really hard.

Anyway, the point is, Fate has obviously decided that my hour of destiny has come. I already have the perfect poem composed and now here is the ideal opportunity for my talent to be discovered and to become a rich and famous world-renowned poet. Well, maybe not rich as I don't think poets make all that much money. Also not famous and world renowned right away as the competition is just for Glasgow Southside schools and the winning entry will just be published in the school's magazine and the *Southside Free Gazette*, but still.

Just think, maybe one day people will have to study my work in Higher English classes. Perfect revenge for all the hours I've had to read boring sonnets.

FRIDAY SEPTEMBER 22ND

Decided my poem is a bit too short so have worked all week on another verse. Think I've got it just about perfect now and have recorded it here as a fitting end to this journal, especially if future scholars one day research my life in order to discover the tragic roots of my moving poetic genius.

G

Oh G, Oh G, Oh G,

Where art thou, Oh G?

Will you ever be

With me?

G?

G

Oh G, Oh G, Oh G,

I still do pine for thee.

Can't you and I be

A 'we',

G?

SaTURDaY SePTeMBeR 23RD

Stephanie has said that to be famous these days you've got to engage a great PR agent and have a scandalous private life to divulge to the press bit by bit. She has offered to be my agent for fifteen percent of all my earnings. She says I should go back to keeping my diary and as soon as my poem is published she would start leaking the juiciest bits.

Told her there weren't any juicy bits yet, which was part of the problem, but Stephanie just looked horrified. She told me that no one writes the truth in diaries these days and told me to start fabricating some interesting five-in-a-bed-romp stuff immediately. She said she'd help with any technical difficulties.

SUNDaY SePTeMBeR 24TH

Liz said I should start writing in my diary again too. She said it was psychologically beneficial and called 'tragic catharsis'. When I asked what that meant she said it meant I could pour out my feelings in my diary instead of constantly moaning the face off her and Stephanie.

Charming.

MONDAY SEPTEMBER 25TH

Stephanie has composed her poem for the competition:

> Come back, Ian, my lusty pig hand lover,
> Give me your willingness and you'll discover,
> With my hand on yours it'll be no surprise,
> Your love for me will grow and thicken and rise.
>
> Come back, Ian, and don't be such a wimp,
> Stay by me and you'll never, ever go limp,
> Thrust yourself in my general direction,
> And I'll take care of your dejection.

TUESDAY SEPTEMBER 26TH

Liz's poem.

> Love is like an illness, an illness of the head,
> If you are rejected,
> Don't feel dejected,
> Just seek professional counselling instead.
>
> Love is like a sickness, a sickness of the mind,
> If you want to stalk,
> Instead take a walk,
> To a psychologist both wise and kind.

Love is like a neurosis, a psychosis most vile,
Good psychoanalysis,
Cures your paralysis,
But it will cost you an enormous great pile.

WEDNESDAY SEPTEMBER 27TH

Don't like to seem unkind or disloyal but given the standard of competition so far, I really feel I could be in with a chance.

THURSDAY SEPTEMBER 28TH

Bollocks, forgot about Graham's stupid parents' visit and, more to the point, my offer to cook dinner until Dad asked how much would I need for the shopping. Hadn't even thought about a menu but just casually answered, 'Oh, around thirty pounds,' in what I hoped was a confident sounding voice then phoned Liz in a panic. At first she wouldn't answer but I left a message on the answering machine promising not to read her one of my new poems and she rang back.

Told Liz about stupidly offering to cook dinner. She said she couldn't believe what an idiot I'd been but finally agreed to help on the understanding that she wouldn't have to read or listen to any more poems, verses, odes, stanzas, whatever I wanted to call them, this year. Had decided to take a break from poetry composition anyway as I felt that my creative juices were beginning to dry up with overuse so told her it was a deal.

Liz came round with some of her mum's recipe books, which we trawled through looking for something simple enough. (We had already decided not to consult Stephanie for help as she was likely to suggest some impossibly complicated *cordon bleu* menu.) Liz suggested that the roast chicken looked cheap and easy but I balked at removing giblets or stuffing things up a bird's bottom so we abandoned that idea. There were a lot of recipes which called for adding tins of condensed soup to grey looking stews but we vetoed those as being a bit minging. The picture of a steak pie that accompanied one recipe looked tasty but making the puff pastry looked too difficult. Liz suggested buying the pastry but then I had a better idea. We could just buy one of those tinned pies you can pop in the oven. It seemed a bit of a cop out but there was no need for anyone to know it wasn't home-made and it was better to be safe than sorry.

For starters we picked prawns with a Marie Rose sauce – even I couldn't fail at that, Liz said, a bit snottily I thought. Still, I needed her advice too much to complain for now. Decided to be more adventurous with the sweet and settled on sticky toffee syrup and treacle surprise.

Even reading the list of ingredients had Liz and me salivating so we went downstairs and finished off a packet of Jaffas.

FRIDAY SEPTEMBER 29TH

Went round to Stephanie's tonight. Liz and Julian were there and Stephanie's boyfriend came round later on. Felt a bit green and hairy even though no one snogged anyone else in front of me. I suppose I'll just have to get used to being the boyfriendless girl in the group. Am rather annoyed with Liz though. I am pretty sure she and Julian have done it by now but instead of telling me all about it she's stonewalling my questions. We had always promised each other that the first one of us to have sex would divulge everything – every single detail – to the other. Instead, she's keeping quiet and just giving me maddening little self-satisfied smiles when I demand to know all. She says that promises made at an earlier stage of social and psychological development don't count. I told her that my promise to lend her my notes for the biology test next week was made at an earlier stage of development too, so tough. Not that I will really not lend them of course but I think I made my point.

Disaster.

Graham's bloody parents came. The father was a skinny, balding little man who looked a bit like Graham – well, I suppose Graham actually looks a bit like him but I saw Graham first even if his dad actually came first – only even less impressive, if that were possible. He seemed to be completely henpecked by his wife and was always looking at her to see what attitude to take on anything. His wife was a really snotty old bat though. She made it obvious from the start that she considered our family a bit beneath her and sat for most of the night with a face like a constipated grouper fish.

Dad tried to break the ice by offering her a drink but she said she 'seldom drank alcohol' and asked for mineral water. The fact we didn't have any, as we weren't stupid enough to pay a fortune for putting tap water in a sodding plastic bottle, was treated by her as confirmation of our low-class status and earned us more snobby looks and sniffs. We also didn't have any fruit juice or lemon tea, and she turned her nose up at Irn Bru or Diet Coke, eventually agreeing with a sigh to, 'Oh well, I suppose a gin and tonic then, this once.'

MNP waddled off to get it, looking pretty worried and sick. Felt a most unusual emotion of sisterly solidarity so followed her to the kitchen and cheered her up by imitating Grouper Face's expression and pretending to spit into the gin and tonic glass.

For someone who 'seldom drinks' Grouper Face fairly knocked it back like a camel and had managed another two in about five minutes flat. At this rate we'd be trailing back and forth to the kitchen all night, so when she asked for another I just brought her the bottle of gin and said, 'Help yourself.' She gave me a nasty look – although it's difficult to be sure as her normal expression is pretty nasty anyway – but took it nonetheless.

Thought I'd better get on with the dinner before the old bat got so drunk we'd have to spoon-feed her. The starter wasn't too bad except that it was a bit crunchy as I'd forgotten to defrost the prawns. We didn't actually have steak and kidney pie for the main meal though, as I'd put it in the oven earlier but didn't realize I was supposed to open the tin lid first, so the bloody thing had exploded and ruined the oven in the process. Fortunately this happened before the arrival of Grouper Face and company so we managed to clear up the mess and Dad arranged for a pal to smuggle in a takeaway of KFC chicken. I just emptied out the buckets onto plates, threw some dried parsley over the chicken, and added slices of lemon. Everyone seemed to like it although Grouper Face commented how much it reminded her of Kentucky Fried Chicken. I just said we never ate that sort of thing and wasn't home cooking so much better and stared her out so she dropped it.

Things seemed to be OK then and everyone was actually starting to talk a bit until the dessert disaster. At first the hot sticky toffee syrup and treacle surprise tasted fantastic as the liquidy sweetness swirled onto the tongue and everyone commented on how good it was. Then they stopped commenting. In fact, they stopped saying anything as the mixture started to cool down and turn chewy and then go solid so that it clamped people's top and bottom teeth together like Superglue. We were all sort of struck dumb, but it was even worse for Grouper Face as four of her top front teeth came out, leaving a large black gap. Dad said later she must have had some dodgy dental bridge work done at some time as real teeth couldn't have just come out like that but whatever, she looked more like a grouper than ever. She and her speechless husband and son left soon after.

A disastrous visit and it's all my fault. It took ages for us all to ungum our teeth and I nipped off to bed before anyone could say anything to me. Can hear MNP crying in her room. Even though she is a pain I still feel horribly guilty. Another awful day.

Dad has just come to see me. He said that replacing the oven would cost £350 and paying for Grouper Face's bridge work would probably set him back another £650. He said that we could all have dined at the bloody Ritz for what this meal had cost him. He also said that it was worth every bloody penny to see the look on the snotty old bag's face when her teeth fell out.

Felt so much better. Really love my dad. Still felt bad about MNP though, who was continuing to cry in her room on and off, and told him so. He said not to be so daft and listen carefully next time so I did.

MNP wasn't crying after all. She was laughing. Had the weirdest sensation of actually almost quite liking my sister for once.

SUNDaY OCTOBeR 1ST

Spoke too soon. MNP reminded me today that I had promised to be her 'back-up birthing partner' and gave me all these gross pamphlets about stages of labour, perineums and placentas to study in preparation. I nodded yes but tossed them in the bin as soon as her back was turned. Unfortunately she spotted them later, when she was throwing out some teabags, and started on about how could I be so irresponsible and selfish, then burst into tears. To shut her up, I've had to fish the bloody things out of the bin, try to clean them up and promise to read them. Now have to look at pictures of cervices streaked with marmalade, tea-stained umbilical cords, and greasy perineums.

MONDay OCTOBeR 2ND

Today we had some mad American woman come to give a talk to the fifth and six years at assembly called 'True Love Waits'. It was basically about not having sex until you get married and how this is a brilliant idea. She said loads of cool young American people are making celibacy vows and how this was the best and safest form of contraception. Couldn't help thinking that having frizzy mouse-brown hair, spots and a flat chest was a great contraceptive and wondering whether I was now the only virgin in the fifth year.

She droned on for ages and everyone had pretty well tuned out by the time she finished up and asked if anyone had any questions.

No one had, except Ms Conner, who had enough for everyone. She kicked off with: was the speaker aware that nine out of ten of the young people who made such celibacy vows later broke them, and that when they did so, they were the ones most likely to have unprotected sexual intercourse, thereby exposing themselves to the possibility of unwanted pregnancy and/or venereal disease? Ms Conner invited the speaker to defend her promotion of a failed abstinence policy that jeopardized the physical, social and emotional health of young people. Giving her no chance to do anything of the sort, Ms Conner ranted on for another twenty minutes until, fortunately for the American who, by this time, looked simultaneously as though she might faint with fear and explode with fury (a weird combination that only a rant from Ms Conner can seem to produce), the bell rang and Mr Smith hurriedly thanked her and dismissed us.

Outside the hall some young American helpers were selling silver rings for a tenner and a pledge of chastity. Stephanie bought one for a laugh from one of the male sellers, promising to be celibate until after four o'clock, when she'd meet him behind the shed and show him what he'd been missing. He accepted eagerly but she stood him up. She says she hasn't got time to mess about with beginners.

WEDNESDAY OCTOBER 4TH

Weird thing happened today. Mrs Atkinson, the art teacher, has asked me to model for her sixth year Advanced Higher class on Friday. Am pretty flattered, I think. Especially as Shelly was really keen to do it but Mrs Atkinson chose me.

THURSDAY OCTOBER 5TH

Mrs Atkinson says Liz and Stephanie are winding me up and I won't have to pose nude – in fact it's just a portrait of my face the class will be sketching. She also says not to worry about spots, that I've hardly got any anyway, and it's my bone structure that's important.

FRIDAY OCTOBER 6TH

Modelling for the art class was totally boring and uncomfortable but Mrs Atkinson let me see the sketches afterwards and I looked really nice in all of them. One of the sixth years called Fraser, whose dad is a photographer, told me if I were a bit taller (well, six or seven inches taller) I could model professionally.

SATURDAY OCTOBER 7TH

Told everyone who would listen (not that many) about Fraser's comments. I said he made me feel like the ugly duckling who'd just turned into a swan.

Chris said, 'You've always been a swan, Kelly Ann.' What a charmer Chris is sometimes. I laughed and told him he could save the cheesy talk with me but that it was a great chat-up line and he should try it out sometime soon. It would definitely work, trust me.

Just wish G would say nice stuff like that to me. Can't see it ever happening though.

SUNDAY OCTOBER 8TH

Has just occurred to me also that perhaps Fraser meant I was skinny and flat-chested enough to be a model. Oh well.

MONDAY OCTOBER 9TH

Really strange thing happened today. G called me at home and said he thought I'd got the wrong idea about him and Shelly, that they weren't really 'exclusive' and that they were just 'seeing' each other rather than going out together. According to G 'seeing' someone means dating them but not just them, whereas 'going out' is seeing only one person.

Anyway, G said that he was really just 'seeing' Shelly but that she was the jealous type and thought he was 'going out' with her. He said he'd like to 'see' me too but we'd have to keep quiet about it with Shelly.

I was a bit confused about the whole thing so just said 'maybe'. I suppose I should feel really happy and excited. After all, I suppose G has just sort of asked me out but I feel a bit flat somehow. He said he'd ring me tomorrow.

TUESDAY OCTOBER 10TH

G rang. I told him I didn't want to 'see' him while he was 'seeing' Shelly. Felt really proud and strong. Liz and Stephanie were really impressed with me, I think. Well, Liz said she'd taken me off 'seriously disturbed' diagnosis to the merely 'a bit mad sometimes' category. Stephanie just said, at long bloody last I'd stopped being a total carpet, which is pretty high praise coming from her. Am sure I've done the right thing.

WEDNESDAY OCTOBER 11TH

What have I done?! How could I have destroyed the chance of winning G? Maybe over time if I'd done everything just perfectly right, he would have realized I'm tons better than Shelly and given her up for me. I've ruined my one chance of true love with my stupid pride.

Almost phoned G but didn't. Don't want to share G with anyone, especially not Shelly.

THURSDAY OCTOBER 12TH

I'll be sixteen in just two days' time. Theoretically G and I could get married then.

FRIDAY OCTOBER 13TH

Asked Dad if I could have a party but he says he's broke. Moaned about it to MNP but she says a party would be too loud for 'baby', that is her foetus (it can hear now apparently), and she only plays stuff like Mozart and Bach to it. Thanks a bunch. So apparently the 'right to life' debate is settled in this house at least. The foetus has rights and I don't.

SATURDAY OCTOBER 14TH

Got a birthday card from Mum that said 'Now You Are Ten' and was signed from Mum and Sergio. Inside was a letter from Mum and £50. The letter said that Sergio had somehow, 'perhaps because he thinks I look so young', got the impression that *I* was also a few years younger than I was and she didn't think it was necessary to correct him over little details just yet. Likewise, she hadn't mentioned MNP and her pregnancy because that was a 'personal family matter' unrelated to her relationship with Sergio. Right.

Anyway, the good news is that Mum is coming home in December and she'll see me then. The bad news is that it's just for a month and she's coming with Sergio.

MNP got me a book entitled *All You Ever Wanted to*

Know About Being a Birthing Buddy and a knitting pattern for baby jackets. Very thoughtful. Not.

Dad had put a lot of thought into my present. Unfortunately it was absolutely the wrong thought. He had the mad notion of buying me clothes. I mean, my dad buying me clothes! I suppose he meant to make up for Mum not being here but if there is one thing even worse than your mum buying you clothes it has to be your dad. He got me this awful outfit. It had a dirndl skirt and peasant blouse with puffed sleeves. Not only that, but it was at least six sizes too big and was covered in embroidery. Had to try it on to please him. He got all misty eyed and told me he'd never seen his 'little girl' look so lovely, then asked me to 'do a twirl', so I had to twirl round like a six-year-old whilst trying to keep a smile pasted to my face. Didn't have the heart to say how awful I thought it was, so ended up having to wear it all day. Liz and Stephanie came over later and nearly wet themselves laughing. Stephanie said I looked like a reject from the *Sound of Music* cast. Hilarious.

Liz had got me a self-help book called *Women Who Love Too Much*, a not very subtle hint that she thinks I still obsess over G too much.

Stephanie then presented me with a gross red see-through g-string which she said was for 'Girls Who Bonk Too Little'. Very funny. Then they gave me chocs and perfume, which were my real presents.

My best gift, however, arrived just after. Sixteen

long-stemmed red roses delivered to my door with a note signed just 'Your Secret Admirer'.

G!!!

Liz and Stephanie of course say not – or 'not that tight tosser' to be exact – but I'm just too happy to let their cynicism touch me.

After Liz and Stephanie left, Aunt Kate and Uncle Jack arrived with a home-baked cake complete with candles. I said I was too old for candles but Aunt Kate said rubbish and made me blow them out and make a wish. You can guess what my wish was but G never appeared, which is probably just as well given the God-awful outfit. Forgot about Uncle Jack's wonderfully sophisticated sense of humour so nearly turned blue trying to put the candles out before realizing that they were joke relighting ones.

It was pretty quiet for such a momentous birthday, I suppose, but I don't care any more. I have my gorgeous roses by the side of my bed and will go to sleep gazing at them and dreaming of G. Oh G, how long will it be before our secret love is declared to all the world? I'm sure you have your reasons for waiting but don't waste too much time, my love.

SUNDAY OCTOBER 15TH

Dreamed of G. We were in the school grounds standing really close and he was moving in to kiss me when suddenly he recoiled in horror. Then I noticed everyone looking at me, pointing and sniggering. I looked down and saw that I was wearing the Von Trapp outfit. Oh God, no!

It was like the nightmares I used to have of suddenly realizing that I had turned up for school naked, only much worse. Must make sure G never sees me in that outfit. Even the strongest love could not survive a test like that.

MONDAY OCTOBER 16TH

No hint from G that he was the one who sent the flowers. Made eye contact with him in assembly and gave him an I-know-it-was-you kind of smile but he just said 'Hi' and asked if he could copy my English interpretation homework.

TUESDAY OCTOBER 17TH

Still nothing from G.

Ms Conner reminded us that the results of the poetry competition were due this afternoon. Had actually forgotten about it by this time. Somehow it seems so much less important now that I know that G is probably my secret admirer. Also Ms Conner has been telling us about Sylvia Plath and I don't fancy having to top myself just to be a famous poet. Have decided instead to be an actress, although if my breasts don't grow a bit more I may have to start out being a 'character actress' instead of just doing those kinds of parts when I'm old.

Was shocked when it was announced that Chris had won the poetry competition. He took some stick from the other boys in the class for winning such a 'girly' competition but he just laughed it off good-naturedly. When Ms Conner read the poem out to us, however, it didn't sound girly or stupid at all. It was quite good in fact, and made me think that Chris really must have wanted some girl like mad and been let down.

Wondered who it could have been. Chris has gone out with a few girls before, but not for long, and he was the one who'd always ended it. Teased him about it at lunch time. He said there was someone but refused to tell me anything else. Thought of asking Liz or Stephanie but they don't know Chris nearly as well as I do, so if I couldn't figure it out there was no chance they'd know.

Poor Chris. Tried to cheer him up by telling him that, though he probably wasn't aware of it, I'd fancied G for ages and thought it was hopeless, but that recently I had reason to believe my feelings might be returned after all.

He didn't seem all that comforted by what I'd said. Just told me, rather nastily I thought, that my feelings for G weren't exactly a state secret, then walked off in a huff. If that's what I get for trying to be caring and sensitive, I don't think I'll bother in future.

WEDNESDAY OCTOBER 18TH

Couldn't hold back any longer. Whispered to G in maths, 'Thanks for the lovely flowers.' At first he pretended not to know what I was talking about, even denying he knew it had been my birthday, but then he just shrugged modestly, said I was welcome, and asked if I had a rubber. Then he said, did I know a rubber was slang for a condom in America?

So it was really definitely true. G *did* send the flowers. Told you so, Liz and Stephanie. G is my secret admirer. Of course, I understand without G having to say a word why he has to keep his feelings secret for now. Obviously G has to wait for the right time and circumstance to confront Shelly with the truth of our love. Naturally she will be devastated to lose G and he must be careful to prepare her in case she has a breakdown or tops herself. He is so sensitive and caring.

But oh G, how you must be suffering with longing for us to be together. Have no fear, I will wait forever for you, My One True Love.

THURSDAY OCTOBER 19TH

Got home from school to find Dad passed out on the sofa surrounded by cans of Tennent's and a bottle of whisky. This is worse than normal as usually he doesn't pass out until around midnight and then only on weekends.

Noticed he was clutching a letter so took it from him and read it as I poured the rest of the booze down the sink. Couldn't understand a word at first with all the wheretofore and hereinafters but finally managed to make out it was a lawyer's letter from Mum about getting a divorce from Dad.

So much for all Mum's talk in the past about lawyers being the scum of the earth, lower than snakes' bellies, and a bunch of sodding ambulance-chasing parasites the lot of them.

Nearly jumped out of my skin when I realized Dad had woken up and was standing behind me. Thought I was for it for pouring away his booze and/or reading his letter but instead he just looked shamefaced and mumbled, 'Sorry, love,' before stumbling off upstairs.

How could Mum do this to Dad? Obviously she had none of G's sensitivity in ending relationships.

FRIDAY OCTOBER 20TH

Stephanie and Liz agree that Dad needs a girlfriend to help him cope with mum's desertion. Liz says that the grieving period must end and Dad should now 'move on'. Stephanie says that all guys go a bit bonkers when they haven't had sex for a while.

Am disgusted with Stephanie's comments. My dad

needs a woman for companionship so he won't be lonely, not anything else. Stephanie said 'Whatever' and offered to look into setting him up with someone. Finally, we all agreed to work on it next week.

SATURDAY OCTOBER 21ST

Went shopping with Stephanie. Couldn't help looking at the middle-aged women in the shopping centre, checking whether or not they had a wedding ring and wondering if they might be suitable for Dad. Stephanie said if I didn't stop staring, people would think I was some sort of mad lesbian with a fetish for older women.

SUNDAY OCTOBER 22ND

Liz suggested using Internet chat sites to find someone for Dad. She says lots of people use the Internet to meet people these days but I didn't fancy the idea. What if Dad agreed to meet someone only to find that his date was actually a sadistic German homosexual who slaughtered him then ate his liver, or worse, an awful Californian woman who was into serial face-lifts, group hugs and the Atkins diet? It was too risky.

In the end we agreed to check out the lonely hearts advertisements in the paper tomorrow.

MONDAY OCTOBER 23RD

Pored over the lonely hearts ads during RE – Mr Dunn said he had a hangover and couldn't be arsed teaching anyone today – but kept getting interrupted at first with some idiots in the class, especially Peter Lynch and Stuart Thomson, who told us if we were that desperate they would be willing to 'give us one' for free. Liz told Peter to sod off and added that the day she was that desperate she would shoot herself in the head, which discouraged them a bit but they finally disappeared when Stephanie accidentally elbowed Stuart in the groin.

Couldn't find anyone quite right for Dad though. Thought that Brenda, the 'bubbly' woman with the GSOH, sounded OK but Liz said 'bubbly' probably meant small and fat while Stephanie thought that anyone who said that they had a GSOH probably didn't.

Finding someone for Dad was going to be more difficult than I thought.

TUESDAY OCTOBER 24TH

Had a brilliant idea. Decided I would raid my breast implant fund – again – and put an advertisement in for Dad. Then we could all scrutinize the replies from the PO box and present him with a shortlist. Oh, and explain what we'd done then too. I'm sure once he sees all the effort we've gone to he'll go along with it.

After a lot of argument – we didn't want any sad 'caring, sincere and likes walks in the country' stuff – finally decided on the wording of the advert.

MALE FORTY PLUS, NOT A TOTAL PSYCHO, WEIRD PERVERT OR COMPLETE SAD LOSER, WOULD LIKE TO MEET SIMILAR FEMALE.

WEDNESDAY OCTOBER 25TH

No letters yet. Liz says we have to be patient, the ad only went in today.

THURSDAY OCTOBER 26TH

Still no replies. Maybe no one wants Dad. Liz said perhaps we should have put caring and sincere in the ad after all but Stephanie said no way. She said no self-respecting woman is going to fancy anyone who says he's caring and sincere.

This worried me a bit because Dad really is caring and sincere but Stephanie said he had to hide it at all costs. She said there would be time enough to confess to character defects later.

FRIDAY OCTOBER 27TH

Couldn't believe it! Dad got a sackload of letters that we dragged back to Stephanie's to read. Liz said there must be a lot of desperate women out there.

Turned out over half of them were young Eastern European women with names like Magda and Olga, who claimed to have fallen instantly in love with Dad after reading his advertisement and wanted to marry him right away although there might be a small delay as visas and passports would have to get sorted.

Once we'd thrown out all the bubblys and GSOHs, as well as some discarded by Stephanie as unsuitable – we were to trust her on these, Dad didn't have that kind of money – there were only a few left.

Was amazed to see that one of them was from Ms Conner. I would have thought she hated men too much to be looking for one. It was a really long letter: twelve pages of small, neat script.

Of course just had to read it although there was absolutely no chance of my ever showing it to Dad. She said that while Dad's advertisement met some minimum requirements she would need a lot more information before deciding whether he was suitable for further consideration. She went on to list 'a number of essential criteria'. Dad would have to be supremely fit and muscular but not a gym bore or sports fanatic. She would expect him to be ambitious and successful but to maintain a proper balance between career and home/leisure time. He would have to be well-informed, have an excellent educational background and love literature; however, he must not be a stuffy academic bookworm and his knowledge of life should be primarily based on first-hand experience. He should be well travelled but not an unreliable globetrotter. A sincere and caring nature was a must; however, he should also possess a hint of excitement and danger about him too. Gave up before I got to the next section listing 'desirable extra qualities'. Began to wonder whether the blonde secretary was the only reason Ms Conner's husband left.

Finally whittled the list down to three. One who listed her main hobby as baking and cake decoration was Liz's and my favourite. Stephanie preferred the woman who worked in Fraser's; the staff discount might come in handy. The third choice was Marianne, who impressed us all by describing herself as having a really poor sense of humour.

Now it was just a matter of telling Dad.

SATURDAY OCTOBER 28TH

Dad introduced me to Betty, a fortyish, dyed (is there any other kind?) blonde who is a barmaid at his local and a 'friend'. He said they'd only just started sort of seeing each other outside of the pub and he hoped I wouldn't be upset about it but he'd been lonely since Mum left and needed someone his own age to talk to.

She seemed quite nice and I'm happy for Dad but can't help being annoyed at plundering my breast implant fund for nothing. Betty didn't look the sort to be interested in baking and it's doubtful whether she would be willing to get me staff discounts for alcohol so it looks like I'm getting absolutely no return on my outlay. Typical.

Dad said he and Betty intended just to stay in and watch a video tonight and didn't I have any plans? Actually I didn't and quite fancied watching a movie but Dad said young people like me should be out enjoying themselves on a Saturday night, not stuck in the house with two old fogeys so I took the hint and cleared off. Couldn't go to Liz's as she and Julian were going out to celebrate their six-and-a-quarter-months-since-they-first-met anniversary. They are getting really couply. Went to Stephanie's instead but Dave was there and I got the impression after a while (like about five seconds) that he and Stephanie had plans for the evening that didn't include my company, especially since Julian and Stephanie's mum were out and they had the house to themselves.

Left early so had to wander round town to kill time before I could go back home. Eventually, on my third circuit of one street, a Salvation Army woman approached and asked if I needed somewhere to stay. Almost took up her offer of a place – it would be nice to feel welcome somewhere – but worried that they might try to enlist me; then I'd have to spend my whole life in a stupid hat and very unattractive uniform, so went home.

Dad and Betty looked pretty close curled up on the sofa so I went to bed and left them alone together. I'd already had enough of playing gooseberry at Stephanie's.

Graham and MNP were in her room. Could just hear MNP droning on about nappies as I passed.

Maybe I'm just turning into a bitter, twisted, jealous spinster. Everyone seems to be a couple now except for me. Sometimes can't help wishing that G wasn't so fantastically noble and sensitive so he could just dump Shelly and be with me. Oh G, how much longer must our love wait?

SUNDaY OCTOBeR 29TH

Don't believe it. Graham has gone and dumped MNP, saying that he needed some 'space and time to think things over'.

Dad is furious. He said, 'Space my arse,' and that Graham should have bloody well thought things over before he got MNP up the duff. Dad said that the real problem was his snotty old trout of a mother and that Graham was too much of a bloody mummy's boy to stand up to her. Dad said Trout Face could keep her mummy's boy and good riddance.

MNP has cried all day. She says she'll now have to be mother, father and grandmother to her poor baby.

She has also promoted me from back-up birthing partner to primary birthing partner. Great.

MONDAY OCTOBER 30TH

If Dad's right maybe it's all my fault and MNP has been abandoned because of the sticky toffee syrup and treacle surprise disaster but Stephanie says not.

She said Graham probably wasn't getting enough sex because MNP was too wrapped up in the pregnancy thing. A fatal mistake, according to Stephanie.

Liz disagreed. She said according to evolutionary psychologists, men are like monkeys or chimpanzees. Once they've got their mate pregnant they lose interest and start looking for non-pregnant mates so that they can spread their genes about as much as possible. However, she said that as humans had developed frontal lobe brains – even men – they should be able to work out that this behaviour was ethically wrong and that MNP should cut Graham's balls off.

Brilliant.

TUESDAY OCTOBER 31ST

Another bloody awful day. First MNP 'reminded' me that her preliminary antenatal class is next Monday and primary birthing partners were expected to attend. Great. Never thought I'd see the day I wanted loser Graham back. Then there was the Halloween party disaster.

Had been so preoccupied with all this Graham stuff that I almost forgot tonight was Halloween. Chris's friend Gary was having the fancy dress party this time. Normally I really love Halloween and every year Liz and I compete for the ugliest, scariest Halloween get-up.

This time Liz's Slowly Rotting Zombie was pretty impressive. She'd used lumps of grey dough tacked to her face, legs and arms with off-white bandages to emulate decomposing flesh but it was the putrefying eye that was the best bit. Liz had hidden one of her eyes with a patch, over which she'd spread some crusted yellow gunge made from a custard and dough mixture. In the centre of this she had stuck a blob of clear jelly streaked lightly with strawberry jam and a plastic fly. The whole thing looked like a gelatinous putrefying eye and was completely gross, especially when Liz later removed some of the jelly with her fingers and ate it.

My own witch's outfit wasn't quite as gross but could easily win – and did – the ugliest Halloween costume of the party award. I'd made the face out of green *papier-mâché*. Everyone said my huge hooked nose with the enormous carbuncle on the end was brilliant. I'd really gone mad too with pustules, boils and warts which covered almost my entire face.

The problem was bloody Gary, who'd invited G this year because although he personally thought G was 'a tosser' he'd been told I liked him. Of course G came with bloody Shelly, who was dressed as a witch too. If wearing a cute pointy hat and black strapless dress while waving around a minuscule plastic broom the size of a pencil could be called dressing as a witch. Bitch had the cheek to tell me how 'fabulous' she thought I looked too.

Liz complimented Shelly sarcastically on her 'imaginative' costume but judging by all the attention Shelly was getting from almost every guy in the room I wished I'd been a bit less imaginative too.

WEDNESDAY NOVEMBER 1ST

Stephanie said not to worry and that Shelly was just a boring slapper. It's all right for Stephanie. She'd looked fantastically sexy in a skin-tight red PVC body suit accessorized with little devil horns, tail and trident. I'd looked, well, like a warty old witch.

Still, Stephanie has told me she's having a huge birthday party at the end of November and it was definitely not fancy dress. Just for me, she has already invited G but told him not to bother bringing the boring slapper and he's said yes. All I had to do now was look gorgeous on the night and my witch costume would be forgotten.

G is coming without Shelly! At last he must have made up his mind to tell her about us, at least before the party anyway. Hallelujah!

THURSDAY NOVEMBER 2ND

Mum still in tears most of the time but at least Dad seems happier. However, woke up early this morning and caught him trying to smuggle Betty out the back door. Gave him a stern lecture about letting girlfriends, well women friends anyway, stay the night. Of course I know that nothing would really go on. Unlike Mum, I'm sure Dad and Betty know they are way too old for that sort of thing and of course I trust them; nonetheless it creates a bad impression and have told him so. I think I made my point.

FRIDAY NOVEMBER 3RD

Liz and Julian are becoming more and more of a romantic couple these days. Julian has bought Liz a gold heart-shaped locket for their six-and-a-quarter-and-a-bit-months anniversary of their first meeting. It has two facing photographs inside of Liz and Julian smiling at each other.

Stephanie's not impressed. She said to pass the sick bag and what was wrong with the pair of them? She said she couldn't believe that her only brother and one of her best friends could be such boring arses and why didn't they play the field a bit more and get a life? But Liz said Stephanie had a cheek to talk. Hadn't she been going out

236

with Dave for ages now and what's more *only* Dave? Liz said it was common knowledge Stephanie had fallen for Dave and hadn't looked at another guy for months.

Stephanie got really mad at that. She said her relationship – if anyone could call it that and she didn't think they could – with Dave was solely based on sex. She said the minute she got bored of sex with Dave he'd be discarded faster than vol-au-vents that had gone off. She said the day she gets sentimental about any guy will be the day she swaps her butterfly thongs and strapless bustier for striped pyjamas and a jacket with sleeves that tie at the back.

Liz and I just looked at one another. So, she really had fallen for Dave then.

SATURDAY NOVEMBER 4TH

Julian is in deep trouble. Apparently a woman had bought her grandmother a Hunky House Husband voucher for her eightieth birthday and Julian got the assignment. The old lady was lovely but worried about Julian catching pneumonia because of her cold kitchen tiles and so made him wear her bed jacket and her late husband's socks whilst he did the washing-up and made a cup of tea.

She was sitting watching the telly in the living room when her son, a local councillor, called round. Being a bit senile she'd forgotten about Julian by this time so her son got a bit of a shock when Julian brought the old lady's tea into the room.

Apparently the councillor thought Julian must have been some kind of a weird pervert burglar so he launched himself at Julian, grappling him to the ground with a rugby tackle and sending the tea tray flying. The old lady then remembered about Julian and started whacking her son with a walking stick, telling him to 'leave that nice lad alone', and look at the mess on her new carpet. Anyway, a neighbour, hearing all the fuss, called the police, who arrested Julian and the councillor for breach of the peace and suspicion of indecent behaviour.

The councillor was furious and kept saying stuff like, this was a disgrace and did they know who he was? The sergeant at the police station said he did know who he was. He was the local councillor who had made numerous official complaints about the slow response time and generally inadequate reaction of local police to residents' complaints concerning noisy, anti-social neighbours. The sergeant hoped that the councillor was impressed by the speed and firmness of the police response on this occasion. The sergeant added that it had been brought to his attention by the arresting officer that the councillor's car had a faulty back indicator light and the tyres looked a little worn and would he like one of his officers to check out whether they met minimum legal standards?

The councillor said not to bother and that the police were very busy people who were doing a fantastic job for the community and that he wouldn't want to put the officers to any further trouble.

Eventually they were both let go with a caution but the councillor has threatened to have Hunky House Husbands shut down.

SUNDAY NOVEMBER 5TH

Guy Fawkes Night. We all (Stephanie, Dave, Liz, Julian, Chris plus a bunch of Chris's friends) went to the fireworks display at the rugby club and for once it didn't rain. The whole school seemed to be there, including G and Shelly, who were standing almost right next to us. Was very annoyed to see them snogging as I didn't think this was the best way for G to prepare her for the eventual end of their relationship. Still, I suppose she must have pressured him into it. Poor G. This must be so hard for him. But not long now until we are together at last and we can tell the whole world of our secret love.

MONDAY NOVEMBER 6TH

Julian has been sacked from Hunky House Husbands. They

claim it's on grounds of incompetence, that is, that he's useless at housework, but Liz says it's because of pressure from the councillor and Julian should take them to an employment tribunal. However, Stephanie says he really is useless at housework so she didn't think he'd stand a chance.

Had to go to MNP's evening antenatal class for first-time mums and birthing partners. There were ten pregnant females, only one of whom had a wedding ring. She quietly slipped it off and dropped it in her bag, so she wouldn't feel out of it, I suppose. Two of the younger ones had their mums with them, the rest had pale and squeamish-looking boyfriends except for one woman with dungarees, short spiky hair and parrot earrings, who I thought had brought her sister, but it turned out she was her lesbian partner.

The midwife, Sister Kline, who was taking the class, was a starchy, scary type who talked to all of us as though we were primary one pupils on our first day at school. Sister Kline made it plain from the start that she was a firm believer in Natural Birth, which she said was Best for Baby and Best for Mum. She told us not to be put off by ignorant scare stories about labour pains; childbirth was a perfectly natural process for which drugs were entirely unnecessary. Any 'discomfort' experienced during labour could be managed perfectly well, she said, with proper breathing, warm baths and massage. It was her aim – and here her gaze swept sternly over each pregnant woman in the room – that all of her antenatal class would 'achieve' natural childbirth.

She droned on for ages after that and I'd switched off till she got to the end and asked if anyone had any questions. Knowing how teachers usually assume you've been listening if you ask a question, and feeling a bit worried she might have noticed I wasn't, I asked the first thing that came into my head – that is, how many children she'd had. She fixed me with a steely glare and hissed something about personal details like that being 'quite irrelevant'. But one of the pregnant girls' mums wasn't fooled and muttered, 'Childless spinster, thought so . . . bloody nerve.'

Then the pregnant lesbian chipped in that she wasn't having any of this natural childbirth bollocks and wanted her epidural booked now.

After that Sister Kline seemed to lose some of her authority. She kept glaring at me for the rest of the session, but I didn't think it was really my fault as all I'd done was to ask her if she'd any children.

After we got home MNP squeezed my hand and said, 'Thanks for coming,' before going off to bed, which made me feel a bit guilty as I hadn't really bothered much about the class or paid her much attention. Wish Mum was here.

TUESDAY NOVEMBER 7TH

Julian is in even deeper trouble. Julian's dad knows the local councillor who's told him about the old lady, Julian's Hunky House Husband job and the arrest. Julian's dad is furious. He says he didn't flog his guts out for years to rear a son who shows his arse to elderly pensioners and thank God the woman had dementia so she'd be able to forget the terrible trauma of her ordeal and not go telling the world about Julian's depraved behaviour. To think that the old woman's husband probably fought in the war so that future generations would be free of flaming fascism, only to find that certain members of those future generations had so little respect for their elders they pranced about practically wagging their bums in elderly widows' faces. Julian was a bloody disgrace and if he didn't pull his socks up and keep his flaming Y-fronts on he was going to be thrown out of the family home without a penny and disinherited to boot. Julian's dad had had enough. Julian was to start doing an honest day's work for an honest day's flaming pay right then. On Monday he'd be employed in his dad's portable toilet business whether he flaming well liked it or not. And Julian needn't think that he'd get any flaming favours because he was the boss's son. Julian would be starting at the bottom for minimum wages and like it.

WEDNESDAY NOVEMBER 8TH

Liz is very upset. Apparently her dad is friendly with the sergeant of the local police, who told him all about Julian's brief arrest. Liz's dad says he's not having his only daughter consorting with what amounted to an effing bloody gigolo and she's not to see him any more even if he has to lock Liz in her room and nail down the bloody windows. He says he's always thought of himself as a fairly indulgent, broad-minded dad but this had gone too far. She wouldn't be seeing Julian again and that was that.

THURSDAY NOVEMBER 9TH

Liz has threatened to go on hunger strike unless her demands to see Julian are met but her dad says a bit of a hunger strike would probably do Liz some good and save him money on the grocery bill as well.

FRIDAY NOVEMBER 10TH

Liz's hunger strike has been temporarily suspended as her dad brought in fish and chips for dinner and Liz couldn't resist the hot vinegary aroma, but she is determined to resume right after supper (three slices of toast, two digestive biscuits and a mug of tea).

SATURDAY NOVEMBER 11TH

Liz is so depressed. Stephanie and I tried our best to comfort her, eventually resorting to Liz's psychological counselling techniques about the stages of grief starting with Denial, etc., but she said to shut it – she didn't need our amateurish psychobabble now.

SUNDAY NOVEMBER 12TH

Liz's mum says if Julian can prove himself in a proper job she would speak to Liz's dad but for now it was non-negotiable. Liz seems more hopeful now but Stephanie has her doubts, which she expressed in typically blunt style as, 'no chance there then'.

MONDAY NOVEMBER 13TH

MNP still cries every night about that stupid bore Graham and Liz is almost always in a bad temper now she can't see Julian. Ms Conner is not much better either and now always brings her terrier, Terry, to class as she fears her ex-husband plans to kidnap the dog due to some sort of ongoing custody dispute. Can't see why either of them wants it, to be honest, as it farts almost continuously so our English class is always bogging.

244

Sometimes I think it would be better if we were all asexual like amoebas or Cliff Richard or something so we wouldn't have all this relationship bother but Stephanie disagrees. She says she's never got the hang of how asexual reproduction is supposed to happen but it sounds bloody boring.

TUESDAY NOVEMBER 14TH

Don't believe it! Stephanie and Dave have split up. Apparently he's confessed that he's not a brickie at all but the son of some big important person in the Foreign Office and that he intends eventually to go to Edinburgh University to study International Law and Business. He said he'd been afraid to tell her in case she went off him.

Stephanie says, too right, she's gone off him. Liz and I agreed with her. How could she possibly trust him after all his lies and deception? Honesty in a relationship was so important. But Stephanie said honesty was bollocks and we were missing the point. She said she just couldn't stand these upper-class academic types. OK, she conceded that whilst labouring during the summer had given him a fit body for now, and she'd been taken in by his cod-common Glasgow accent, she liked a genuine bit of rough. Trust her, she knew these types. In a few years Dave would be a pale, skinny shadow of his former self who raised his pinkie when sipping tea, always had a sherry at six o'clock exactly and spoke in a high nasal whine. No way.

WEDNESDAY NOVEMBER 15TH

Dave has sent Stephanie about five hundred begging texts, left fifty voice messages on her mobile and emailed her incessantly but she is adamant she won't see him.

THURSDAY NOVEMBER 16TH

Dave has texted Stephanie to say that she is a stupid stuck-up reverse-snob bitch and he wouldn't take her back if she begged him. Stephanie has said that's fine by her.

FRIDAY NOVEMBER 17TH

Stephanie says she's not in the slightest upset, why should she be? Yes, the sex had been OK, she'd give him that, but there were plenty more where he came from and she was looking forward to trying out new talent.

Was relieved that Stephanie wasn't going to be all tear-ful and pathetic like MNP or bad-tempered like Liz so invited her round to my place to watch a video. Had been really looking forward to a girlie Friday night with Stephanie as she'd always been with Dave lately but spoke too soon.

The movie was great. I'd never heard of the lead actor before but he was totally fit and spent most of the beginning of the film striding about the jungles of South America stripped to the waist and carrying a submachine gun in muscular arms but Stephanie wasn't impressed. First she remarked that the actor's body wasn't a patch on Dave's and I was surprised to hear her voice catch a bit and see tears forming at the corner of her eyes. Then she barked that she didn't want to watch any more of the stupid film anyway and was going off home. Great. Obviously Stephanie's reaction to the break-up was going to be tears *and* temper. Bloody fantastic.

SATURDAY NOVEMBER 18TH

Mum called. Dad answered the phone but she wouldn't speak to him and just asked for me. She said that she and Sergio would be in Glasgow on the first of December and she'd see me on the second. She asked about my spots and bra size (not too bad and a B cup, sort of, now) but didn't ask about Dad or MNP.

Dad was really quiet all day after the call and didn't even ask what we'd talked about but I lied anyway and said Mum had asked after him and MNP. MNP burst into tears and said she didn't believe me – Mum didn't care about her or her baby. Dad said nothing until after dinner (fish and chips again, which no one ate) when he told us he was going to see Betty.

Thank God, at least he's got her to cheer him up.

Stephanie, Liz and Chris all rang to suggest going out tonight but with MNP still sobbing in her bedroom I decided I'd better stay in and see she was OK. Took a cup of tea and a chocolate biscuit up to her bedroom and endured a long baby talk, this time about the relative merits of various kinds of leak-proof disposable nappies versus environmentally friendly terry towelling ones, which are apparently coming back into fashion. Managed to convince her, I hope, that pails of minging nappies around the house wouldn't be a brilliant idea and steered her firmly in the direction of disposables.

Talking about the nappies seemed to cheer her up anyway, so decided it was OK to go back downstairs and watch some television. Was a bit embarrassed but also touched when MNP clutched my hand before I left her and said that I was the best sister she'd ever had.

Took me a little while to work out that wasn't much of a compliment.

SUNDAY NOVEMBER 19TH

Dad said that he'd finished with Betty. He says he's still in love with Mum and it wasn't fair on Betty to lead her on like this.

Bollocks.

Why does Dad have to be so decent and sincere? Stephanie's right, it's a real character problem. Wish couples could manage to stay together for longer than five minutes too.

MONDAY NOVEMBER 20TH

Chris suggested going to see a movie after school but I told him I had to get back to see if Dad was OK. I was worried he'd start drinking heavily again now that he and Betty were finished.

Dad seemed OK, if a bit quiet when he got back, but when Chris called again to see if I wanted to see the later showing, I thought it best to stay in and keep an eye on Dad, although I just said I couldn't be bothered as I didn't want Dad to overhear me. Was pretty surprised when Chris arrived at the door fifteen minutes later and said to get my coat, he was taking me out whether I liked it or not and I shouldn't be staying in all the time like this. Chris can be extremely stubborn sometimes and anyway Dad heard him and shooed me out.

Had a really good night. The film was a hilarious comedy and afterwards we went for pizza, which was great. Don't know why, then, I should have started blubbing like an idiot on the way home. Chris gave me a tissue and a hug but otherwise didn't say anything. Felt much better when I'd finished crying but was a bit embarrassed too. Fortunately, I don't think anyone saw me, and Chris promised not to tell anyone about it.

TUESDAY NOVEMBER 21ST

Fantastic day. Guess what? G and Shelly are over. She found out he was going to Stephanie's party without her and went spare. G told her she was a boring, jealous cow and she was dumped. Hurray! At last a split that's completely good news. Of course I know that G wanted to find a more sensitive way to end the relationship but her ridiculous behaviour made that impossible. Poor G.

Anyway, even better, G called me after school and said not to forget our 'date' on Saturday night at Stephanie's. Am so happy I could burst! It's really going to happen this time. I can just feel it.

Oh G, Oh G, Oh, Gggggggg!!!

WEDNESDAY NOVEMBER 22ND

Feel awful. In my selfish bubble of bliss about G and Saturday night I had totally forgotten about Liz's problem. As she is banned from seeing Julian, her dad says she can't go to Stephanie's party.

Stephanie has suggested that Liz quickly finds a string of truly awful boyfriends to introduce to her dad so that he will see things could be worse than Julian and so relent.

I recommended the goth in the sixth year who calls himself Damien the Damned but everyone else knows as Alex. Since the second year Alex has refused to wear the school uniform, favouring instead a floor-length black coat which he wears all the time, even in PE. Although originally fair he keeps his hair permanently dyed jet black, which looks even blacker because of the contrast with the white make-up on his face. Alex is a member of some weird vampire club and he is always boasting that he goes for walks every night in graveyards where he confers with tormented spirits of the damned.

Perfect.

There was no time for Liz to seduce him so she just offered him a fiver to meet her parents that night posing as her boyfriend. Alex said material stuff like money meant nothing to him; however, he'd do it in exchange for a CD. Liz was pretty annoyed as this would cost her much more than five pounds but was so desperate she agreed.

Turned out to be a total waste of money. Liz called to say her parents seemed totally cool about him. Her dad said of the vampire society and graveyard walks that it was good for Damien to have an absorbing hobby. As for Liz's mum, apparently she remembered him as Alex from a mother and toddler group she had gone to with Liz years ago. She said Alex had been a very cute wee boy who loved *Thomas the Tank Engine* but was virtually the last to be potty trained. She told 'Alex, sorry Damien' to mind and tell his mother she was asking about her and that they must have coffee one day.

THURSDAY NOVEMBER 23RD

This time Liz invited a total ned called Billy the Bam who always wears gross lime green trackies, carries a baseball bat for 'protection' and is subject to several anti-social behaviour orders. However, to Liz's fury, he made a special effort to impress her parents and couldn't have been more polite and respectful all night. Liz's parents said what a nice young man he was and Billy the Bam told Liz that her parents were 'pure quality, man'. Liz's parents say he can visit any time.

FRIDAY NOVEMBER 24TH

Liz's last-ditch attempt involved inviting Georgiana, otherwise known as George, who is an incredibly butch, built-like-a-tank lesbian. George turned up wearing leather biker gear and with her usual array of tongue, lip and forehead studs as well as tasteless tattoos on every bit of exposed flesh. Liz sat on the sofa with George, holding hands and giving her looks of simpering adoration.

Liz's parents said later that of course they expected a period of experimentation in adolescence but at the end of the day, Liz's sexual orientation was a matter for her.

Then they said that they were well aware of what Liz's recent ploys had been about and not to try their patience or insult their intelligence any longer. They said, however, that she could go to Stephanie's party after all but not to think that this was permission for her and Julian to go out together again, because it wasn't. Julian would have to prove to them that he could hold down a responsible job and behave in a decent, socially acceptable manner before they would change their minds.

Liz is ecstatic about the party but a bit concerned about George, who seems to have developed a fancy for her, judging by the three times she called Liz after leaving the house. She's offered to take Liz to the pictures, and buy her an all-you-can-eat mega lunch at Pizza Hut. Liz was quite tempted by the lunch.

Saturday November 25th

10:00 am
D-Day – or G-day anyway. This is my day of destiny. Woke up this morning and didn't have a single spot. Feel it's a sign that my hour has come. Tonight will be the night G and I will declare our secret love. Am going to spend the entire day making myself beautiful for the most important occasion of my entire life. Just know everything is going to work out fantastically well. For the first time in my life I feel totally confident, beautiful, powerful and serene. Oh G, just a few more hours and you'll be mine.

1:00 pm
Have just read my horoscope. It said that Venus is square with Uranus and this means that the outlook for love is poor. What should I do? Maybe I shouldn't go tonight in case it's a bad time.

1:30 pm
Phoned Stephanie in a panic and got the expected cheap 'Uranus my arse' joke but she did give me some good advice. She told me to check out another horoscope, so I did. The *Daily Post* said tonight Mars was in conjunction with Venus, which made it a fantastic night for romance. Hurrah!

2:30 pm

Have just checked out a third horoscope to make sure and it wasn't quite so good. It said that with the new moon in my opposite house and Neptune opposed by Venus and Mars, deception and conflict were possible and I needed to be very careful in my dealings with others. Maybe I should look up some more horoscopes.

5:00 pm

Julian has emailed me a list of 200,000 horoscope websites. Have checked over fifty of them and they all seem to be different. Don't know what to do now.

6:00 pm

Liz came round. She said horoscopes were superstitious rubbish and not to pay any attention to them but she has lent me her lucky silver locket, which she says is virtually guaranteed to bring good fortune in love.

7:30 pm

Think Liz's locket is working already. Have never looked better. Stephanie has lent me a short, red, strappy dress, which she says is a little too tight for her but fits me perfectly. For once my skin is flawless without a single spot, blemish or pimple, just a few freckles, but can't do anything about that. Liz helped me straighten my hair with her new straighteners and now it shines in the light. Liz said I looked fantastic and would have to fight guys off with a stick tonight. She said it's just a pity it was all going to get wasted on G.

Am so happy. Just know that tonight will be the best night of my life.

SUNDAY NOVEMBER 26TH

What a weird night last night. Of course I feel ecstatically happy but also somehow really upset. It's all Chris's fault.

Stephanie's party was amazing, of course. She had invited hundreds of people, there was a real live band who could actually play, and best of all her mum and boyfriend had booked into a hotel for the night so we were free to do what we wanted. There was lots to drink, of course, but the food was a bit tasteless – loads of smoked salmon, vol-au-vents and crudités – so some of the boys went off and brought back chips, pizza and curry carry-outs. I was too excited to eat though and didn't have much time either, as practically everyone wanted to dance with me.

Stephanie and Liz had warned me not to focus on G all the time and though he followed me round all night, for once I took their advice and danced and flirted with loads of other people. And it worked. G couldn't take his eyes off me and kept trying to get me to himself.

It was round midnight when the lights were dimmed and the band started to play a slow number. Actually it was a pretty awful old song, 'Lady in Red', which my mum used to like before she went mad, but still, it was the first slow dance and I could see G making a bee-line for me from across the room. I caught his eye, smiled and waited.

Was really annoyed then when Chris unexpectedly came up beside me, put his arm round my shoulder, and said, 'C'mon, Kelly Ann, I requested this one for you. Let's dance.'

Couldn't think of an excuse so found myself shuffling round the floor with Chris whilst trying to keep an eye on G by peering over his shoulder. Good. He hadn't asked anyone else to dance and was still looking at me.

When the dance finished I immediately started to hurry back towards G but Chris caught my arm and said he needed to talk to me. What was it now? Could see that Chris's face was all serious so I supposed it had to be really important. Maybe the kitchen was on fire, someone had fallen from a top-floor window or worse, all the drink had run out.

Went with Chris upstairs to Stephanie's room, which amazingly was not occupied by any couples having it off. Mind you, Stephanie had warned everyone that her room was off limits and had threatened to toss out starkers anyone found bonking in it.

Chris just looked at me but said nothing at first, so I really started to panic that it was something truly awful he had to tell me. Horrible thoughts popped into my head. Perhaps Chris was seriously ill and had only six months to live. Or maybe my mum had posed nude on the Internet for some dreadful website like hornyhouse-wives.com and Chris was trying to break the news to me before everyone else knew about it.

Was both relieved and annoyed when Chris finally spoke to say that he had to tell me that he really liked me.

I mean, big deal. Of course he liked me. We were friends. Began to suspect that Chris was drunk but he appeared to be totally sober.

But then he said that he meant that he *really* liked me. That he thought I was beautiful and that he'd fancied me for years. He said he wanted me to be his girlfriend and not just a girl who was a friend.

Was totally gobsmacked. Who'd ever have imagined that Chris fancied me? This was awful. I didn't know what to say but Chris was obviously expecting some sort of reply. Really wished he hadn't told me all this now.

Had to tell him that though I liked him as a friend I didn't think of him in 'that way'. Also pointed out that he must know that I was totally in love with G. He nodded at that but looked gutted. I said I hoped we would still be friends but he said, no, we couldn't be friends any more because he fancied me too much and it was tearing him apart. He would have to move on.

Just at that moment the bedroom door opened. G! He didn't come in straight away but leaned against the doorframe and asked what the two of us were up to. Chris said, nothing – he was just going, then he looked at me and said, 'Goodbye, Kelly Ann,' in a really sad and final kind of way before walking out past G.

G came in then and shut the bedroom door. We moved towards each other and then it happened. I was in G's arms and he was kissing me. It was absolutely fantastic of course, except that G's breath smelled strongly of beer and the chips with curry sauce he'd had earlier. Also, I was still a bit upset over Chris.

We snogged for quite a long time, then G was so overcome with passion for me that he pulled me down onto Stephanie's bed with him and tried to pull my dress off. G is so romantically impulsive! However, I told him that now was not the right time to give full and ultimate expression to our feelings. He said that I was right enough. He'd heard Stephanie goes spare if anyone but her has it off in her bed and that maybe we should invite her to join us, ha ha. We went back to join the party. Saw loads of people looking at me when I danced with G and felt so proud until Liz came up and whispered to me that the back of my dress was tucked into my knickers.

Still, it was a fantastic night and G is mine at last. I am absolutely ecstatically blissfully happy. I really am. And I am not going to let this stupid business with Chris spoil things for me. Definitely not.

MONDAY NOVEMBER 27TH

Everyone in the school knows that G and I are together. Not only have I finally got a boyfriend but it's G, the most gorgeous guy in the whole school.

We met up and went out for chips at lunch time. Was a bit embarrassed when he snogged me while waiting in the queue but it is kind of flattering too that he just can't seem to keep his hands off me. Felt bad though when Chris walked by. I broke off and said 'Hi' to Chris but he just nodded and walked on.

G has invited me to his house tomorrow at seven to have something to eat and maybe check out his new PlayStation game. Our first real date. Was so happy I nearly kissed the lollipop lady on my way home.

TUESDAY NOVEMBER 28TH

Was a bit disappointed that something to eat was six Jammie Dodger biscuits and a can of Coke (he'd already had dinner). Afterwards G invited me up to his room to see his PlayStation. Instead he was again overcome by passion for me. However, this time I was wearing tight jeans so I was able to control the situation a bit more.

Gently I explained to him that a first date was too soon for us to express the ultimate consummation of our love for each other.

G asked, 'How many dates before it's OK to shag then?'

Was pretty stumped by this. Didn't want to give in too early or he might not respect me and I could be a 'pump and dump' victim. On the other hand if I didn't have sex with him soon enough maybe he'd get fed up and go off with someone else. Also, being a virgin I didn't know if I'd be any good at it. Briefly wondered if I should get in some practice with someone else first but supposed it was too late now. Finally said, 'Seven.'

He said OK so long as tonight counted as one.

WEDNESDAY NOVEMBER 29TH

Wondered if having sex for the first time was painful. Asked Stephanie but she couldn't remember as it was so long ago. Asked Liz but she wasn't giving anything away. Finally, believe it or not, asked MNP. She said as long as the boy was gentle, sensitive and patient then it shouldn't be painful. Boring Graham had just gone up a bit in my estimation and I told her so but she snapped, 'Who said it was Graham?'

THURSDAY NOVEMBER 30TH

Chris is going out with Linda. Am happy for him of course and relieved not to feel so guilty but feel a bit annoyed too. I mean, after saying how much he'd wanted me for years he wasn't very long in getting over me really. Also I miss Chris a lot. Somehow I feel a bit empty without him as my friend. Wish things would just go back to the way they were.

FRIDAY DECEMBER 1ST

Ms Conner has decided that the school Christmas performance this year will be an alternative nativity play.

Instead of being set in Bethlehem two thousand years ago, the play will tell the story of a single pregnant teenager in the East End of Glasgow who cannot find suitable accommodation because of the paucity of council housing stock and instead has to stay in a bed and breakfast run by a ruthless, fraudulent, private landlord who manipulates the benefit system by charging exorbitant rents for substandard accommodation.

Instead of the usual nativity stable, the teenager is forced to give birth on a trolley in the corridor of a chronically underfunded NHS hospital where junior doctors have to work hundred-hour weeks and nurses are constantly cleaning up vomit left by aggressive drunks who wander in at all hours of the night and day.

There would be three wise women from the Women's Refuge Voluntary Association bearing useful gifts such as nappies, babygros and educational toys. In place of shepherds gazing at the baby, women from the Women's Organic Allotment Promotion would supply the mother with healthy fruit and vegetables as well as eggs from free-range corn-fed chickens.

Apparently Mr Smith isn't pleased. He says Christmas is a time for tradition and anyway, what about God in all this? Ms Conner says this is a play of gritty existential realism and that therefore there was no place in it for Judaeo-Christian mythology. As for Christmas tradition, she would be happy to discuss with Mr Smith the myriad traditions associated with this season throughout different cultures and centuries. For example, the Roman Saturnalia was typically celebrated with public disorder and wild orgies, but she didn't think it would be suitable for an end of term play – however, if Mr Smith wanted to discuss the feasibility of various options . . .

Mr Smith didn't.

Liz has been cast as the pregnant teenager but she isn't flattered to have been chosen as the alternative Madonna. She says she thinks it's because she's put on weight lately. I am one of the nurses who gets to clean up the vomit. Great. Only good thing is G gets to play a drunk so with any luck we'll be able to work together. Chris, of course, is a doctor, while Stephanie is going to do costume design.

* * *

Went to the pictures with G tonight. He kissed me good-bye at the end of the night then whispered, 'Just five more to go.'

saTURDaY DeCeMBeR 2ND

2:00 pm
Can't put off thinking about it any more. I have to meet my mum and Sergio this evening at his brother's restaurant. Am so mad at Mum yet I really want to see her again. Don't want to meet Sergio at all. I hate him. Just wish he would go away so Mum would get back with Dad. Feel like I'm some sort of envoy for the family, although neither MNP nor Dad has said a word to me about it. Can't believe I'm nervous about meeting my own mum – but I am.

11:00 pm
Sergio was drop-dead gorgeous, genuinely keen on Mum and very likeable. Hate him more than ever. Dad has absolutely no chance.

SUNDAY DECEMBER 3RD

Felt really depressed today, which is odd as I wouldn't have ever thought I could feel bad and be G's girlfriend.

I really miss Chris. He was the only person I could talk to about Mum. Decided to call him and try to sort things out so we could be friends again. He didn't answer his mobile so phoned his home number. His mum answered and I thought at first he wasn't going to come to the phone as he took so long when she called him, but he did.

I said that obviously he'd been extremely drunk on the night of the party and had said a lot of stupid stuff he really didn't mean and that I could understand he was feeling embarrassed now. However, I explained to him that I hadn't taken any of it seriously at all. In fact I'd actually forgotten most of what he'd said and there was no reason why we couldn't just be friends again like we'd always been.

But it didn't work. In fact Chris sounded really angry with me. He said that he hadn't been drunk, that he'd been totally sober in fact. He told me that he had meant every word he'd said even if I didn't remember it. Then he said that it wouldn't be a good idea for us to meet up for a long time.

Chris can be a stubborn, pompous ass at times.

G phoned and suggested we meet up but I was getting a bit worried about using up my date ration before researching this sex thing so I stayed in and did just that. Looked in some of my school biology textbooks first but they just went on about stuff like fallopian tubes and seminal vesicles so they were pretty useless. Thought about asking Stephanie again but decided that her knowledge was too advanced. I needed something a lot more basic, so to speak. Liz tended to stay annoyingly secretive about her experiences and in any case I would probably just set her off about how much she was missing Julian.

Tried typing 'sex' into Google but got about two million hits, all of which were totally disgusting. Really don't know how you are supposed to find out beginners' rules, like where to put your knickers once you've taken them off and what to talk about whilst a guy is putting on a condom.

Decided to phone Stephanie and ask. Should have known better as just got facetious suggestions such as 'on your head' and 'marmalade making'.

Hilarious.

MONDay DeCeMBeR 4TH

Liz is really worried about Julian. Apparently he's been texting and emailing her constantly saying that he hates his job and is thinking of packing it in. She's begged him to stick it out for a bit longer so her parents will eventually let them get back together.

She let me see a sample of his emails. They were longer than *War and Peace* so I didn't attempt to read them properly. Did notice that he addressed Liz by the name 'Sugar Plum Fairy' and signed off as 'Vlad the Impaler' but Liz refused to go into any details about the meaning of these truly cheesy nicknames.

Got me thinking though whether G had a special personal name for me. Shouldn't have asked. Turns out to be 'Seven'.

TUESDAY DECEMBER 5TH

Liz and I are really worried about Stephanie. She hasn't had a boyfriend since her split with Dave and apparently this is her longest period without a date since her tenth birthday. She says she just seems to have lost interest in guys recently. She's tried looking at video clips and posters of all her favourite hottest actors and footballers but nothing seems to get her going any more.

WEDNESDAY DECEMBER 6TH

Went over to G's tonight. We watched television in the living room for a while. Before I left, G gave me a quick kiss at the door. Then he whispered, 'Three down, only four more to go.'

THURSDAY DECEMBER 7TH

Am beginning to really worry about this sex thing. Asked Liz when the right time to have sex with a boyfriend was. She said if it's bloody G, then never. Very funny. Not.

The response from Stephanie was also typical. She said mornings were good because guys were at their randiest then. On the other hand, sex at night guaranteed a good night's sleep afterwards. Her personal favourite, however, was the afternoon. In summer she liked to do it outdoors, but in the winter the back seat of cars was fun. Then she said our little talk had helped to bring her sex drive back and she was going to try looking at those posters and video clips again.

Eventually took the desperate decision to ask MNP. She said I should only have sex with a boy when I felt the time was right and when there was mutual trust between us. Then she added, flushing a bit, that I should also sort out contraceptive protection. Finally she took a paperback book from the bottom of her underwear drawer and handed it to me. It was called *Joyful But Responsible Sex*. Before I left she tried to give me a sisterly hug but we couldn't connect because of her bump.

MNP isn't quite as stupid as I thought. She'd given me brilliant advice. Obviously the time was right as I was already over the legal age for sex and virtually everyone in my year, including my two best friends, had done it. Also, how could G ever trust me again if I didn't keep my promise about having sex with him by our seventh date?

Had a skim through MNP's book. It had lots of fuzzy black and white sketches of a naked couple (the guy had a beard so you always knew which one was male) doing it in various positions. Spent the rest of the evening trying out some of these positions (well, the female bit, anyway) in front of a mirror to see how I looked. Discovered I'd have to start at a more advanced level than the missionary position as my breasts looked too flat like that. One pose, which involved getting on my hands and knees, was great for making the most of what I had but only if the guy was on all fours facing me and I didn't think sex would be possible like that. Viewing myself from this angle it occurred to me that for once I was glad that Mum wasn't here so she couldn't do her usual barging in at the wrong moment.

Have decided to see G on Friday, Saturday and Sunday then it's . . . position 21, page 60, I think.

FRIDAY DECEMBER 8TH

Bollocks. Couldn't meet G, or not for a date anyway. Had forgotten Ms Conner had organized an evening rehearsal for her stupid play. Worse. She's decided that to add 'interest to the narrative', Chris and I are supposed to be having some torrid affair at the hospital and will have to have a snogging scene at some point. I mean, how embarrassing is that? Linda was furious as she's a nurse too. She complained to Ms Conner but was told pretty sharpish exactly who was, and who was emphatically not, in charge of casting. Linda spent the rest of the night scowling at me as though the whole thing was my fault. Honestly, someone should tell her that ridiculous jealousy is very unattractive.

SATURDAY DECEMBER 9TH

MnP asked if I'd go Christmas shopping with her. Didn't like to say no, as she was now the size and shape of a giant Teletubby and would probably need help carrying stuff, but it turned out to be much worse than I imagined, especially as we had to stop every ten minutes to look for a loo.

By the time we got home I was so knackered I fell asleep on the couch. Didn't wake up until eight o'clock, when Dad told me G had rung and that he'd said to G I couldn't come to the phone as I was lying on the couch with my mouth open, drooling and snoring loudly.

Very funny.

Apparently G's gone out without me anyway. At this rate I'll be an old age pensioner by the time we have sex.

SUNDAY DECEMBER 10TH

Stephanie and Julian are meeting their dad for dinner tonight at the Marriott. Apparently it's Danielle's twenty-fourth birthday and her dad wants them all to celebrate together. Stephanie has persuaded her dad to invite me too.

Never been anywhere so posh. Felt a bit intimidated by it all, especially when it came to ordering food, so just said I'd have the same as Danielle. Definite mistake. Even though it was her birthday, and any normal person would want to pig out, Danielle had only ordered melon balls and asparagus tips for her starter, a plate of green leafy stuff with three prawns and six walnuts (I counted) for a so-called main course and no dessert! Stephanie said it's called 'cuisine minceur'. Yeah, right. Won't be having that again. It wouldn't satisfy an anorexic hamster on appetite suppressants.

Stephanie's dad spent most of the meal banging on about some virus that had infected the computers at his business and was affecting productivity. Julian was trying to fix things but so far without success. Julian explained the virus was contained in an email called Why-Bother-Working-When-Your-Boss-Is-A-Lazy-Rich-Tosser that some workers had opened in error, believing it to be a bona fide business communication. Once in the system, the virus did no direct damage but merely searched the human resource files for details of senior executives' earnings then displayed these along with a program facility which could show the figures as a ratio of a particular employee's own wages. Finally, there was a feature that automatically downloaded all the coolest Internet games available. Apparently some staff then spent most of their day playing around with these games instead of getting on with their work.

Stephanie's dad is furious about the whole thing and said the law was too soft on hackers, who were nothing but hooligans. He said that the creator of this particular piece of virus vandalism should be bloody well hung as an example to the rest of them.

Julian agreed, saying, 'You're right, Dad, bloody well hung.'

All in all, I was glad when the meal was over and Stephanie's dad dropped me back home. Was still absolutely ravenous so had to ask my dad to nip out and get me sausage and chips from the chippy. He seemed a bit taken aback given he knew I'd been out for a meal but just asked if fish or chicken would do if they had no sausages. I just told him anything would do so long as it wasn't 'cuisine minceur'.

TUESDAY DECEMBER 12TH

Still haven't managed to see G. This time it was Liz's fault. Apparently she has told her parents that she is on hunger strike again in protest at their ban on her seeing Julian although she also secretly thought it would motivate her to lose weight. But tonight she was desperately hungry and could I come over and smuggle in some food so her parents didn't know she'd given in?

Was met at the door by Liz's parents, who put on mock worried faces and whispered something about how Liz was now into the third hour of her hunger strike but they thought she'd survive at least till morning. Hilarious. Bet Liz's parents are the type who would describe themselves as having a GSOH in lonely hearts advertisements.

Got a bit of a shock when I went into Liz's room though. She was lying on top of the bed, illuminated only by a dimmed bedside light. She looked very pale and there were dark shadows under her eyes. However, when she saw it was me, she got up and turned on the room light so that I could see that her face was covered with pale foundation and that she'd dabbed dark blue eyeshadow underneath her eyes.

As we ate the stuff I'd brought – chicken sandwiches, crisps and chocolate – we talked about how Julian was getting on working for his dad and I mentioned the virus thing. She said she'd heard about it and that it had been on the news that night. Apparently the virus has spread all over the Internet and productivity has plummeted in almost every developed country. She said that it was so bad that Scotland Yard, Interpol and the CIA are all trying to hunt down the hacker responsible.

Noticed Liz looked a bit down and worried, so to cheer us up I suggested we put on cucumber face masks and watch Liz's *Dirty Dancing* DVD.

It worked and soon we were singing along to the music and dancing about like mad things on top of Liz's bed with our faces covered in pale green stuff. We must have been making so much racket that we didn't hear her dad knock and come in. He just said that he was glad she was feeling a little better and did we want him to bin the crisp packets and chocolate wrappers?

WEDNESDAY DECEMBER 13TH

At last got to see G. He had obviously missed me and was impatient for us to show the ultimate commitment to our relationship but typically he hid his true feelings and desires under a mask of humour, just asking where the hell had I been all week, and saying that if he didn't have sex soon, his tadger would fall off with lack of use.

Was able to tell G that on Saturday evening my dad and MNP would both be out so we'd have the house to ourselves. Have also told him that this was the evening I wanted to give myself to him completely and utterly so that we could be as one, united in body and soul for ever.

G said, great, he'd bring a condom then.

THURSDAY DECEMBER 14TH

Had double English today. Ms Conner's dog Terry is still in class and the stench from it is getting almost unbearable. Don't know how Mr Dunn can pretend to like it the way he does just to get in with her. Have heard of people being blinded by love but not losing their sense of smell for God's sake. Mind you, it seems to be working as Ms Conner has definitely warmed to Mr Dunn and been impressed by the fact that the thing always runs to him when he comes near. Actually heard Ms Conner say to Mr Dunn today that a dog really needs a man about the house and how difficult it was for her to make this up to Terry. According to Melanie, who has a little sister in the second year, Mr Dunn kept smiling for the rest of the afternoon, thereby totally terrifying the two second year RE classes he had after lunch.

After school G asked to see me in order to make up the required number of dates but I told him that our love should not be dictated by numbers; rather it should be a spontaneous outpouring of our deepest feelings and as such independent of time, space and frequency. Also I had too much homework this week, including a punishment exercise from Ms Conner for making a derogatory remark about her smelly dog.

G said, fair enough, he'd see me Saturday at seven and he would come prepared. Then he winked, took out a small package from his top blazer pocket and waved it in front of me.

Sensitive, passionate and responsible too. I am so lucky.

FRIDAY DECEMBER 15TH

Am so excited. Just think, this time tomorrow I will no longer be a young naïve girl but a grown woman who has experienced love for the first time. Also feel a bit nervous. What if I do something wrong and G thinks I'm some sort of idiot?

Stephanie says not to be stupid. She says I should just get drunk – she would if she were bonking G – and it will be all over and done with without me even knowing about it.

Liz says I'm suffering from performance anxiety. She gave me some tips on reducing stress such as muscle relaxation, deep breathing and self-hypnosis exercises. Then she advised me just to get drunk – she would if she were doing it with G. Hilarious.

SATURDAY DECEMBER 16TH

Can hardly bear to record this day but it was meant to be a momentous occasion so can hardly leave it out.

Got up late, around midday. Decided to wash my sheets in preparation. To stop Dad and MNP suspecting anything, I also did towels, woollens and a general wash.

Later, when it was time for me to get ready, I couldn't get into the bathroom as, unusually, Dad was hogging it for ages, showering, shaving and brushing his teeth. When he finally came out, I dived into the shower only to be forced out again thirty seconds later as MNP needed to pee. Have told Dad a hundred times since MNP got pregnant that we need another toilet.

Finally MNP and Dad left. MNP was spending the evening at Aunt Kate's, being fitted for a maternity Christmas dress and discussing nursery decoration. Personally I'd rather have spent the evening having my nails pulled out with pliers but she seemed happy enough. Dad had said he was just going to the pub with some pals from work so I thought it a bit odd when he asked MNP and me whether he looked OK. Hope Mum hasn't put him off women so much he's thinking of having a gay relationship with one of his pals. Am trying to be broadminded but don't think I could handle my dad having a boyfriend right now.

Managed to get ready just five minutes before G arrived. As soon as we went into the living room and shut the door, G showed how madly attractive he found me by immediately pushing me onto the couch, lunging on top of me and trying to pull my T-shirt off.

I was flattered, of course, but felt a bit panicky too and decided I needed to take Liz and Stephanie's advice about alcohol. Not that I'd get really drunk, of course (the thought of spewing up before, during or after sex didn't appeal), but just a small drink to relax us would be nice.

Murmured to G in what I hoped was a classy American-movie-star voice that I would 'go fix us a drink', but he didn't seem to hear me, perhaps because my T-shirt was now over my head so muffling my voice. Had to knee G in the abs to get his attention but must have overdone it a bit as he fell off the couch.

Went into the kitchen and made us two vodkas and Cokes. Was a bit shocked on my return to the living room to find G sitting on the sofa stripped to his boxers and dangling a green condom in front of me. Might possibly have found this sexy if it hadn't been for the colour of the condom. As it was I found myself trying to suppress a fit of the giggles. I mean, why green? Maybe it was his lucky colour.

G says not. He told me the condoms were going cheap if bought in bulk and so he'd purchased a gross for ten pounds ninety-nine. He winked cheekily and said he intended to use at least a fiver's worth tonight, then patted the space on the sofa beside him.

Just then the doorbell rang. G told me to ignore it – it was probably Jehovah's Witnesses – but I couldn't relax until I knew who it was. Shooed G into the kitchen and went to answer the door, rehearsing my usual 'I am a Charismatic Catholic/fundamental Muslim/Orthodox Jew and therefore not interested in religious conversion', in case it was actually Jehovah's Witnesses.

Chris! He said he wanted to talk then brushed past me, through the hall and straight into the living room. He told me he'd been thinking over what I'd said last Wednesday and that he realized he'd been immature and just plain wrong in his attitude. He said that he valued our relationship and missed me. He asked if I would forgive him for rejecting my offer of friendship, which he was now ready to accept if I was still willing.

Was ready to say fine, yeah, cool, see ya tomorrow, when G, understandably impatient, emerged from the kitchen, and said, what was that tosser doing here and why didn't I just tell that sad loser swot to piss off?

Whilst I do really love G, I was annoyed at him speaking about Chris like that and was about to tell him that Chris wasn't a swot but just fantastically intelligent, when Chris launched himself at G, toppling him to the ground. Then he pinned G's arms to the floor and told him that if he ever spoke to him like that again, he'd beat him to a pulp.

I was furious with Chris for physically attacking G and rushed over to pull him off by yanking Chris's hair back and yelling at him to let G go.

Was so caught up in the crisis and noise that I failed to hear the front door open and Dad come in. Learned later that he'd forgotten his wallet but the first I knew of his arrival was when he said, 'Jesus Christ, what the **** is going on here?'

Dad ordered Chris and G out right away although he

eventually allowed G to put his clothes on first. Then he told me that I had some explaining to do and that he considered honesty between a father and daughter very important to their relationship.

Told Dad that G had been walking near our house when he was splashed by a bus and his clothes got all muddy. He knocked on our door and asked if he could use our washing machine to clean his clothes before any stains took hold and I'd said yes. G then went into the kitchen, stripped off his clothes and put them in the wash.

Meanwhile Chris came over to return a CD he'd borrowed and I'd gone upstairs to my room to put it back when G, realizing Chris was in the next room, came out for a bit of a chat. Unfortunately Chris accidentally stumbled on a bit of uneven carpet and fell over G. Hearing the commotion, I had rushed down and tried to help Chris up when, well, that's when Dad had come in. Thinking quickly, I added that, as luck would have it, G had actually taken the precaution of carrying with him a set of clean clothes in case he got splashed but had forgotten all about it until told to get dressed by Dad.

Dad looked at me for a hideously long moment, then said he was glad that I agreed with him on the importance of honesty between a father and daughter to their relationship. He said it should be avoided at all costs.

He collected his wallet from the coffee table, scanned the room briefly and said that it looked like it had been a busy night for visitors right enough. It seemed that some randy Martian had been here as well and left a green condom on the floor. Messy bugger! But Dad was glad to know extraterrestrials practised safe sex too.

SUNDay DeCeMBeR 17TH

Chris called. He said he was sorry about all the commotion and asked if things were OK with me and my dad. He said he was serious about still wanting to be friends, so what did I say?

Told him that he would have to apologize to G first and that I thought it was disgraceful to physically threaten G like he did, and some doctor he was going to be if he went around beating people up instead of curing them.

Chris said, 'Hell would freeze over' before he'd apologize to 'that total tosser'. So we left it there.

Called G, who was pretty cool about things. He blamed that sad loser Chris for the whole fiasco and promised we'd get together soon. After all, he still had one hundred and forty-three condoms left.

So that's what a gross is.

MONDay DeCeMBeR 18TH

8:00 am
Bloody dress rehearsal tonight. That's all I need. A love

scene with Chris when I'd like to slap him.

11:30 pm
Whole evening was a disaster.

For a start my nurse's costume, made by Stephanie, was a joke. The flared skirt was so short it showed my knickers and the low-cut bodice was so tight I could hardly breathe. Stephanie had also provided me with a push-up bra that gave even me the appearance of having a cleavage. Stephanie told me it was the same type of bra used by Julia Roberts in the *Erin Brockovich* movie and wasn't it fantastic? Was so gobsmacked by the transformation that Stephanie had breezed off to see to someone else before I could complain that I looked like a total slut.

Later Stephanie asked me to take a bucket of fake vomit out on stage to G. Got the expected whistles and catcalls – 'Hey, Kelly Ann, you've forgotten your skirt' and 'Nice knickers' etc. – from the usual sleazers and ignored them. But was dead pleased when G took the bucket from me and whispered how fantastically sexy I looked.

Ms Conner told everyone to be quiet then instructed G to do his 'drunk vomiting in the accident and emergency waiting room' scene. Stephanie had made the fake sick from a mixture of cold chow mein and vegetable soup. It looked disgustingly realistic when G stuffed the mixture into his mouth and expelled it forcibly onto the floor. So realistic that everyone was totally grossed out when Ms Conner's dog trotted out on stage and ate it.

Then it was the bit I'd been dreading all night. Chris and I had to go out and do the passionate clinches in the sluice room scene. Of course no one seemed to have anything better to do right then than stand around and watch us, so ensuring absolute maximum embarrassment.

At first we were both really awkward. Chris put his hands on my shoulders while my arms remained limply by my side then we pressed our lips together briefly.

Ms Conner was not satisfied. She said she'd seen more passion at a trainspotters' convention. She reminded Chris that he was supposed to be locked in a passionate clinch with a beautiful young nurse, not kissing his elderly maiden aunt. She told me I was supposed to be to be snogging a handsome young doctor who I couldn't keep my hands off, not embracing a giant sea slug with halitosis. She said to do it again.

This time Chris put his arms round my waist and I put mine on his shoulders and we kissed for a bit longer but Ms Conner was almost as scathing. She said OK, this time Chris might have been kissing a *favourite* maiden aunt, and as for me, the giant sea slug had perhaps used mouthwash but it was still not good enough and we'd repeat the scene until we jolly well got it right.

Tried to point out to Ms Conner that it was really difficult to do a passionate clinch when Chris and I weren't an item but she got pretty snappish with me. 'It's called acting, Kelly Ann. Acting. That's what playing a scene is all about.'

Chris whispered to me, 'Let's just get it over with,' and then he pulled me towards him. Embarrassed, I arched away from him but he held me close and pushed me up against the backstage wall so I couldn't back away. Then he kissed me full on the mouth and I had that fluttery butterflies-in-the-tummy feeling that I'd had when Chris kissed me on the Paris holiday, only this time followed by total fury at his making a complete show of us. There was loud applause from our 'audience', along with wolf-whistles and stupid comments like, 'More', 'Way to go', and 'For God's sake someone throw a bucket of water over them.'

Heard Ms Conner shush everyone up and remind them that this was a serious gritty play with important social connotations. I decided the only thing to do was just to go along with it by pretending to be all overcome with exaggerated passion too, rather than look like a total prissy idiot. Of course, when I got Chris alone later he'd get a black eye. So when Chris pulled me away from the stage wall a little and then started to run the fingers of one hand through my hair and trace the outline of my face and neck, I closed my eyes, threw my head back dramatically and feigned sighs of lust.

But then his other hand was caressing my thigh and moving up to the hem of my skirt. Next he was kissing my neck and shoulders and caressing my inner thighs, sweeping up from the backs of my knees to the tops of my legs.

I began to feel all fuzzy, hot and breathless, and was dimly aware of someone moaning but didn't realize until later it was me. Heard Ms Conner say, 'Excellent, well done, perfect,' but didn't register what she was talking about and didn't care. The only thing that seemed to matter was how fantastic I felt and how I never wanted the feeling to stop. It was as though the world was just Chris and me and everyone else had faded away. There was no Ms Conner, no Liz, no Stephanie, no G.

G! What was I doing? Chris was going to ruin everything. I shoved him away sharpish and stumbled to the front of the stage. Where was G? Oh my God, he'd left in disgust. It was over.

Frantic now, I asked Ms Conner where he'd gone. She said he'd gone to the toilets five minutes ago and she hoped he wasn't smoking there, but never mind him just now, my performance had been excellent and I had real potential as an actress. Chris had come up behind me and Ms Conner beamed at him. His performance had been 'outstanding' and had he ever considered a career on the stage?

But Chris wasn't listening to her. He told me he needed to talk to me in private but I said no. Then he said OK, we'd discuss things 'right here and now', so I agreed to give him just two minutes in private.

We went to the cloakroom, which was empty. Chris

started by saying that he knew I must feel something for him or I couldn't have responded to him like I had but I told him sarcastically that it was called 'acting, Chris. That's what you do when you play a scene.' But Chris wouldn't believe me so I told him all I'd done was just to imagine I'd been kissing G so had got 'a bit carried away'.

Chris looked pretty gutted and asked me if I really meant that. I said I did, so then he just walked away without another word.

Really hate Chris for upsetting me like this. Am not going to let him spoil things between G and me.

TUESDAY DECEMBER 19TH

5:00 pm

Amazing thing happened today. At the end of school we were all streaming out when Ms Conner's ex-husband and his blonde secretary swept into the school car park in a new BMW. Then the husband got out and confronted Ms Conner, who was walking towards her car with Terry on a leash. Ms Conner's ex brandished some documents at her and demanded that she hand over the dog as the courts had granted him sole custody.

We were all gobsmacked when Ms Conner started to cry. Had never seen her display the slightest weakness, never mind crying. Then Mr Dunn came striding up like Schwarzenegger in *The Terminator*. He told Ms

Conner's ex to stuff his papers up his you-know-what (although 'you-know-what' wasn't exactly what he said) and that if he didn't get into his car and push off right then, Mr Dunn would personally put him back in said car without bothering about opening any doors beforehand.

The ex muttered something about Mr Dunn being welcome to the bad-tempered snappish little thing, and the farty dog as well, then got into his car and drove off sharpish.

Ms Conner looked well impressed with Mr Dunn. Wonder if she'll let him sit near her at the school dance tonight as they are two of the teachers meant to be supervising us.

Can't wait for the school dance. This will be the first time I've gone to one with my very own boyfriend.

1:00 am

Unfortunately G didn't make the school dance so I decided not to go either. His friend Johnny said he'd come down with a migraine but Liz said she'd been told G had got so tanked up after school on two bottles of cider that he'd passed out. Don't know why Liz is always so bloody nasty about G. Put her hostility down to her frustration at not seeing Julian.

Stephanie texted to say that she didn't much enjoy the dance although Ms Conner and Mr Dunn certainly did. Apparently they spent almost the whole time smooching surreptitiously (or so they thought) in the cloakroom. Suppose it will be back to boring bloody love sonnets next term then.

Stephanie also said that Chris and Linda weren't at the party either and the word is that they are finished, although no one knows who dumped who.

G texted me after the dance saying he was OK now. Looking back on it I'm sure I was so turned on by the scene with Chris because I'd been thinking about G and am frustrated that we've not yet had sex. Am determined to do it with him before the actual play on Thursday. Dad is out tomorrow although MNP will be in. Still, she just keeps to her bedroom all evening these days, only coming out to pee. Have decided to sneak G into my bedroom and finally do it.

WEDNESDAY 20TH DECEMBER

The evening didn't go exactly as planned.

Dad went out again after showing more unusual interest in his clothes and grooming but I hadn't time to worry about that. MNP was in her room by eight o'clock and G came over at nine. We pretended to watch telly in the living room for an hour or so then, when I thought MNP had fallen asleep, we sneaked upstairs to my bed-room and put out the lights. G stripped down to his boxers straight away and got into bed but I was too embarrassed so joined him under the covers still wearing my long T-shirt as well as bra and knickers.

Seemed really strange to have an actual guy in my bed instead of my usual Gerry the giraffe. Felt so sophisticated and grown up but also a bit scared too. We started snogging but I was feeling really nervous and tense, which caused G to complain that he felt as though he was trying to do it with a shop mannequin so I decided to close my eyes and concentrate on breathing deeply to calm my nerves. G obviously misinterpreted this as he said, 'Bloody hell, Kelly Ann, don't tell me you've fallen asleep.'

Reassured him that I hadn't, that the deep breathing was passion, so we carried on and I'd even let G take my T-shirt off when MNP burst in and turned on the light. She stood in the doorway in a short nightie and peed on the floor like the possessed daughter in *The Exorcist*.

MNP screamed that her 'waters' had broken and she had started labour. G sprang out of bed like it was on fire, saying he was getting out of there. He got dressed at the speed of light and raced off.

I put my clothes on whilst trying to call Dad on his mobile but as usual he'd switched it off. Phoned Aunt Kate's but they were out so I left a garbled message on the answerphone. Then tried to call a taxi to take us to the hospital but either the numbers were engaged or they didn't answer. Bollocks.

Suggested to MNP that we call 999 and get an

ambulance but she had calmed down a lot and said she thought she might be able to hang on for a bit. She said emergency calls were just for heart attacks and road accidents. MNP suggested that we walk to the nearest taxi rank and get a black cab from there. It was only fifteen minutes and maybe we could flag one down on the way.

MNP shoved on a coat over her nightie, put on shoes and gloves then handed me the hospital bag that she'd had neatly packed and ready for the last six months.

Walking to the taxi rank was a big mistake. After just five minutes she had to stop and lean on a wall as she was racked with strong, painful contractions. Frantic now, I looked for any passing taxis but they were all full and hurtled past. Finally in desperation I leaped out in front of a passing motorist; who screeched to an emergency stop then got out of his car to swear at me. Meanwhile, motorists behind him were having to swerve to overtake on the outside lane and giving him and me rude gestures.

Without a word to the car owner I grabbed MNP, shoved her towards the back of his car and bundled her in, then squeezed in beside her with her bag propped on my lap. Then I told him if he didn't get us to the hospital quickly she would have the baby right there and what would that do to his nice clean car upholstery?

He got in and raced off like he was in the Grand Prix, depositing us at the hospital entrance in five minutes flat.

Was so relieved when the hospital staff took over and

whisked MNP off to the labour room while I had a Coke and flicked through some ten-year-old magazines in the waiting area. Had just got to the pattern for crocheting a tea cosy when a nurse came up to me and said MNP was ready for her birthing partner now. Shit.

MNP was sitting up in bed, screaming. Wasn't sure what to do but decided I was definitely going to position myself at the top end of the bed so I went up and a bit awkwardly held her hand. Big mistake. She clutched my hand in an iron grip, digging her nails into my palm as she screamed again with another contraction.

Trying to be helpful I suggested she try to 'remember your breathing relaxation exercises' but she said, screw that, she was in agony and to tell these effing nurses to effing well give her pethidine and an effing epidural or she'd batter them with their own effing forceps.

Was totally shocked to hear MNP talk that way but the midwives didn't seem to be bothered by her outburst and, after telling her that it was too late for that as her baby was coming, they just continued to chat about the party they would be going to when their shift was over.

I apologized for her anyway but they said not to worry, they were used to this sort of language in the labour ward and MNP's outburst was pretty mild.

MNP continued to shriek like a tormented soul with each push and dug her nails deeper into my hand so that I was nearly begging for pethidine myself but then, after one huge push and scream, the nurse said the head was out.

Just the head! Jesus, how long was the rest of it going to take? But amazingly the rest slithered out about thirty seconds later and MNP was holding a wet, red, crumpled creature, which the nurses said was a boy, across her chest, and gazing at his cross face as though he was some gorgeous new guy she'd just fallen for.

After a little while, MNP asked if I wanted to hold it but looking at its slippery body, I politely declined.

However, a bit later, the nurses cleaned it up and wrapped it in a towel thing so I agreed to carry it to its cot. Had just got hold of it when the door of the labour room opened and I heard a familiar voice telling me to put that baby down, I wasn't holding it right, and I'd probably drop the poor thing on its head.

Mum! . . . And Dad!

Mum took the baby from me and started crooning to it in a ridiculous high-pitched voice but the baby seemed to like it and fell fast asleep. Couldn't help noticing that Dad had his arm round Mum's waist as she was rocking the baby and Mum wasn't objecting. Then Mum passed the baby to Dad and went to sit beside MNP and talked to her quietly.

I whispered to Dad, 'What's going on with Mum? Is she coming back?'

Dad said, 'Maybe, we'll see.'

At least he hadn't said 'Maybe later', which in parent-speak means absolutely no chance. Anyway, looking at his face, which seemed happy for the first time in months,

I was pretty sure at last that things were going to work out just fine.

THURSDAY DECEMBER 21ST

Didn't go to school today or turn up for the play because of all the family excitement. Ms Conner was very disappointed but said she understood.

Mum has admitted that she had been going through a mid-life crisis and Dad has said that he had made things worse by not paying her enough attention. They both say that they are going to work on their marriage more.

Told them that I hoped this didn't mean they were going to start snogging at home but they have promised not to, at least not in front of me.

Mum also told Aunt Kate that the strain of living with a toy boy had got too much for her. She had been getting up every day before dawn to put on all her make-up and was constantly having to suck in her tummy (so much so that she nearly passed out for lack of oxygen on several occasions).

When she explained all this to Sergio on the day she left him, he'd pleaded with her to stay, saying that he loved her wrinkles and 'little round jelly belly' and was bored with all the young women with perfect complexions and flat abdomens who were constantly coming on to him. However, this only made Mum more determined to go back to Dad.

Mum called Graham, who was at his mother's house. I heard her tell him that he was a pathetic excuse for a man and not nearly good enough for her daughter but that, given he was the father of her grandson, he'd better get his sorry backside over here pronto or there would be trouble and she hoped she didn't have to spell out what kind of trouble but to take it from her that he wouldn't be fathering any more children, legitimate or otherwise and to put his mother on the phone.

Then she talked to Grouper Face. Mum told her that her son was a pathetic mummy's boy and not nearly good enough for her daughter. However, given that her son was the father of Mum's grandchild, he had better shift his arse up here in the very immediate future or they would both (Graham and Grouper Face) wish that Graham had never been born.

It was so great to have Mum back.

FRIDAY DECEMBER 22ND

Graham arrived today. He's told Dad that he had felt a bit left out of it with MNP so focused on the baby but that he did love her and wanted to get back together. He told Dad that he intended to stand up to his mum more in the future and that his loyalties were now with MNP and his baby.

Dad told Graham that was fine but not to ever think of

trying to stand up to his future mother-in-law. Graham said it had never entered his head.

SATURDAY DECEMBER 23RD

The Why-Bother-Working-When-Your-Boss-Is-A-Lazy-Rich-Tosser hacker has been found. Agents from Scotland Yard, Interpol and the CIA have swooped on Julian's house, arrested him and confiscated his computers.

Liz is distraught and blames her parents for forcing him to stay in a boring job where he had to turn to hacking out of desperation. She is preparing the psychological case for his defence.

SUNDAY DECEMBER 24TH

Julian has been offered jobs with Scotland Yard, Interpol and the CIA as well as several top computer companies and finance firms. He's thinking them over.

Liz's parents have said that she can see him again provided he doesn't take the CIA job.

MONDAY DECEMBER 25TH
CHRISTMAS DAY

Most fabulous Christmas ever even if shared with bawling infant (imaginatively named Graham Junior), dull Graham, boring MnP, drunken parents and equally pissed aunt and uncle. OK, especially since shared with all of above.

My best present was a WAP camera phone from Dad although Aunt Kate didn't approve, saying it might make me a target for paedophiles. Pointed out that I was too old to interest paedophiles now but that didn't seem to stop her ranting on. Nothing does.

Stuffed myself to bursting point on turkey, Christmas pudding and chocolates. When I couldn't force even one more After Eight down and had listened to 'White Christmas', which is Aunt Kate's favourite, for the umpteenth time, I decided to drag myself off to bed.

G had given me a picture frame complete with a photo of himself looking fantastically sexy, which I've put on the table beside my bed. Tried lying on the bed holding it above me and slowly lowering it to my lips but the lack of a third dimension made it a rather disappointing experience.

Despite our fall-out Chris had posted me a present. It was a brown teddy bear with a cute face and large yellow bow round its neck. Thought of putting G's picture over the teddy's face and then lowering both slowly towards me so as to get over the two dimensional problem but that seemed a bit disloyal to Chris as well as seriously weird so just tucked the teddy into bed with me.

Wish Chris and I could be friends again – then everything in my life would be perfect. We've fallen out loads of times before, of course, but we've always made up again.

TUESDAY DECEMBER 26TH

Went over to Chris's house. Seemed odd to feel nervous about visiting Chris but he said he was pleased to see me and invited me in. His house was packed with relatives so we went up to his bedroom.

Normally I would have sat on the bed with my legs tucked under me but suddenly self conscious now, I perched on a chair while he leaned against his computer desk.

I thanked him for the teddy. He said I was welcome and thanked me for the CD. Then I asked him if he'd had a nice Christmas and he said that he had and asked about mine. I said that it had been great, thanks.

Silence. This was awful. Couldn't believe how awkward and stilted I was with Chris now. Just wanted to go, so told him I'd be off then. Got up and headed for the door but, as I attempted to open it, Chris had come behind me and with one hand held it shut.

He said, 'Why don't you just tell me why you've come here, Kelly Ann?'

Turned round to face him and was suddenly very conscious of how close he was to me. So close in fact that I could see each individual hair on his arm, which I focused on rather than looking him in the face, and even close enough to feel the heat from his body which I found unsettling. Also, being trapped between Chris and the door reminded me of that stupid play and how I'd felt when we were kissing on stage. Now I was uncomfortably aware of him as a guy, instead of just a pal, and found myself even thinking mad stuff like what a good body Chris had and what it might be like to snog him for real.

This was all wrong. Obviously frustration at not yet managing to have sex with G was driving me mental and causing all these deranged thoughts about Chris, who I've known from primary school for God's sake. I mean, get a grip. Was determined to get on with what I'd gone there to say and quickly, especially since I needed him to move away from me as soon as possible.

Told him that I wanted him to apologize to G so we could be friends again and it wouldn't be awkward when I was dating G.

He took his hand from the door, moved back and said, 'OK.'

I said, 'Yeah, right,' I knew the kind of apology he was talking about, the 'sorry that you're such a tosser, G' variety and did he think that I was an idiot or something?

But Chris said that he would apologize properly to G.

He said that he'd been thinking things over for some time, that my friendship meant a lot to him, and if apologizing to G was what it took to keep it then he would do it.

Great, now all I had to do was sort things with G.

Was a bit surprised to see Shelly at G's house but G said she was just collecting some CDs she'd loaned him and that one of the things he really liked about me was that I was really mature about relationships and wasn't the type to be jealous about old friends stopping by.

Was thrilled to know how highly G thought of me. Also it was a great time to tell him about Chris. G said, fine, whatever, but that the apology had better be good.

Am so happy. Now I can have G and Chris. They'll probably even become best friends. Maybe G will ask Chris to be best man at our wedding one day and possibly even godfather to our first child. Then I thought about MNP's scary labour and decided to forget about the godfather bit.

WEDNESDAY DECEMBER 27TH

Can't believe it. Stephanie has given in and contacted Dave. She says they can get together again on condition that he's willing to visit the gym five times a week, go labouring at the weekends and only ever drink pints of Tennent's lager with un-raised pinkies.

Dave has said he's willing to do all of it but is refusing to have sex with her until she says she likes him.

Stephanie told him that of course she liked him, that he had a fabulous body and the sex was great, but Dave says that isn't what he meant and she knew it. Unless Stephanie was willing to admit she had feelings for him that start above her waist it was over.

Stephanie told Dave that once, after they'd had sex, there was a fleeting moment when she might have felt she quite liked having him around even when she wasn't feeling randy.

Dave said that was good enough for him, he'd be round in half an hour to see if they could recapture the fleeting moment.

THURSDAY DECEMBER 28TH

Great news. MNP, Graham and infant will be going to Graham's grandmother in Edinburgh first thing tomorrow whilst Mum and Dad will be staying the night at Aunt Kate's.

At last G and I can be alone together! Am determined to finally consummate our relationship. Called G to tell him but he said there was no way he was going to risk bonking in my house again. He said you can't move in my house for swots flying into mad rages, fathers trying to toss people naked out in the streets and sisters bloody well determined to have babies on the bedroom floor no matter who happens to be shagging there at the time. G says just the thought of trying to bonk in my house was enough to shrivel his tadger and that he'd rather have sex in Argyle Street in the rush hour than try to do it at my place.

But then G said his parents were off tomorrow evening to visit his gran in Ayrshire until after New Year. He'd told them that he would rather do a ten-year stretch in Barlinnie, including slopping out, than spend a week at his gran's in Ayrshire and that he'd stay here and look after the house. After various threats of what they would do to G if so much as a toothpaste smudge in the sink was spoiling the appearance of the house on their return, they agreed.

G was going to kick off by having a party tomorrow. He said even if all seventy people he'd invited so far came we'd probably have more privacy in his bedroom than we'd managed in my house so far. Then he said I could invite who I liked, including Chris, who could do his apology stuff then.

Liz said that G's aversion to doing it in my home was a fascinating example of classical conditioning overriding the fundamental sex drive, which just went to show that behaviourists were right and Freudians wrong. However, on the other hand, it might be an archetypal case of classic Freudian repression. It was all very complex really.

Stephanie said that was bollocks and there was

absolutely nothing complex or repressed about G.

Liz asked if I was going to finally do it with G tomorrow. Told her I was and that I didn't feel quite as nervous about it now as I'd had two sort-of dummy runs already. Liz said 'dummy' was the word but then she made me promise to tell her every detail about it. Stephanie said just to use my camera phone and text messaging to give a more blow-by-blow account.

Then we started ringing round people inviting them to G's party. By the time we'd finished we had more people coming than G but Chris wasn't keen at first. Reminded him of his promise so he eventually agreed.

FRIDay DECEMBER 29TH

Just checked my horoscope. It said tonight Venus, Mars and Neptune were in conjunction and so it was a fabulous night for love. Well, one of the horoscopes did.

SaTURDay DECEMBER 30TH

Liz phoned this morning and asked if I'd done it and if so she demanded to know every detail as promised.

Told Liz that promises made at an earlier stage of social and psychological development don't count and I wouldn't be telling her anything. Revenge at last.

Last night was the most amazing night of my life although almost nothing turned out as I'd planned or expected.

Went early to G's to help out with arrangements, which was just as well as G and his pals had done nothing. Took me two hours to get things ready, by which time it was eight o'clock and people started to arrive, at first in twos and threes, then whole groups at a time. By half past nine nearly everyone had come, G was belting out the music and people were busy getting pissed although not yet making total arses of themselves.

Couldn't see any sign of Chris and was beginning to worry that he had changed his mind and wouldn't be coming but then Liz reminded me that Chris always kept his promises and so barring accidental death he'd be here, nothing surer.

It was nearly ten o'clock before Chris finally appeared. G had gone out with Billy and Johnny's big brother (who was eighteen) to the off-licence to get more booze before they shut and so I had used the opportunity to put on my music from the *Top Gun* soundtrack (G hated it). My favourite, 'Take My Breath Away', was playing when I spotted Chris coming in the door from the hallway. He gestured 'Hi' then made his way towards me through the crowded room.

Couldn't help noticing that loads of the girls were eyeing him up. Suppose it wasn't surprising really given that

Chris is actually a very good-looking guy. However, he didn't seem to notice the attention he was getting and came straight up to me then kissed me lightly on the cheek. He asked where G was, so I told him then I said: 'Dance with me.'

Chris gave me a mock salute, I suppose because I had sounded so bossy, but he took both my hands in his and led me to the dance bit of the floor. He held me at some distance at first but I closed my eyes then pulled him closer to me. Chris said something about not teasing him but I ignored him. I really wanted, needed, these few minutes with him. As we danced, all I could think about was how good it felt to be touching Chris again. Familiar but strange, safe yet at the same time somehow new and dangerous. Wow, talk about Take My Breath Away.

I reached up on tiptoes, meaning just to bring my face close to his, but soon I was kissing him for real, not thinking or caring about what anyone thought or how it looked, just wanting to stay like this for ever.

Suddenly the music stopped mid-song. Heard G say, 'Who the hell put this crap on?'

There were groans and complaints from loads of people but also roars of approval from others. I sprang apart guiltily from Chris right away. With the music dead, my mad feelings for him seemed to disappear along with it. What on earth had I been thinking of getting all romantic and sexy about Chris? What was the matter with me? How could I have thought about Chris in that way when this was the night, of all nights, I should be thinking of no one else but G?

It was stupid. G was the most fit, fantastic guy in the school and tonight he'd be mine completely. OK, so maybe he wasn't the most romantic boyfriend ever and perhaps he could be just a bit selfish sometimes but it was G I wanted, not Chris. Of course it was.

But G had seen us and was totally pissed off. He came right up to me and said what did I think I was doing snogging Chris as soon as his back was turned, and then, speaking to Chris and me, he said we could both just push off and take the crappy film music with us.

By this time the whole room had gone quiet and everyone was staring at us. I didn't know what to say or how to fix things. My dream of being G's girlfriend was over and it was my own stupid fault. Felt tears starting to form in my eyes but fought them back as things were bad enough without everyone seeing me with black mascara streaks running down my cheeks.

Then I heard Chris saying that G had it all wrong. That he and I were just good friends and that everyone knew it was G I'd always wanted. We'd just been exchanging a friendly kiss and there was no more to it than that and wasn't that right, Kelly Ann? He apologized to G about the other night and hoped that G wouldn't mind the two of us continuing to be friends as everyone knew I didn't fancy him at all and would no more go out with him for real than I'd snog my own brother if I had one.

G seemed to calm down a bit then and even slipped an arm round my waist. He told Chris he'd think about it but that he should just push off in the mean time.

Chris reddened a bit at that, which is usually a prelude to him losing his temper, but he just said, 'Bye, Kelly Ann, I hope we'll always be friends.'

After he moved away someone put some music on and everyone went back to what they'd been doing. Mainly getting drunk.

G gave me a beery, slobbery kiss, pushing his tongue so far down my throat that I almost gagged. Suddenly I realized that I didn't always like G's kisses. In fact, the thought occurred to me that I wasn't really sure sometimes whether I liked G all that much. I mean, when had he ever really cared about how I felt or done anything just to please me? And he was forever eyeing other girls up, even now, I noticed, while he was snogging me. I pushed G away from me but he didn't even seem to notice I was annoyed. He just smiled at me, patted me on the bum and told me to go fetch him a drink from the kitchen as he was going over to talk to Shelly for a while. I stood where I was and watched him go and basically hit on Shelly, who certainly wasn't objecting. That was it, the absolute last straw. Stephanie and Liz were right. G was a total tosser and I'd just wasted a whole year of my life chasing after him.

Meanwhile, Chris was leaving and I knew for sure that I didn't want him to go – not without me anyway. I scanned the room frantically for him. Had he gone already? But no, I could see him talking to Stephanie and Liz. It looked like he was saying his goodbyes to them but they were trying to persuade him to stay. Stephanie was holding onto his arm while Liz was offering him beer, which he was refusing. Then Chris was shaking off Stephanie and turning to leave. Probably it was too late now but I had to try anyway.

I yelled, 'Chris, stop.'

Chris turned round.

I rushed over to him, pushing past people standing in my way, not caring that they probably thought I'd gone absolutely mental by now.

When I reached him I gabbled, 'I don't want to be friends with you any more—'

'Right, that's fantastic, Kelly Ann,' Chris interrupted. 'I've just made a total idiot of myself in front of your tosser of a boyfriend for nothing. Of course it has to be said that making an idiot of myself over you is nothing new. I've been doing it for years. And by the way, your boyfriend has just left the room with Shelly so you'd better check up on him soon. Don't say anything else. And I mean nothing. I'm going.'

'– because I fancy you too much.'

Chris didn't say anything. Just looked at me. I babbled on anyway. I said I'd fancied him since Paris really but just didn't know it until about . . . er . . . two minutes ago, although the kiss on stage was very, very exciting and I hadn't really been thinking about G at all then. I'd just said I had and I didn't really know why I'd said that. And I was sorry I'd lied to him. Anyway, I knew for sure now that I wanted him more than anybody else in my entire life including G who *was* a tosser actually and did he still want me?

Chris said, 'You're too late, Kelly Ann.' And I wanted to die right there, but then he went on, 'For the last direct bus to your house but we could get a taxi or walk maybe. It isn't that far and we've an awful lot to . . . erm . . . talk about on the way.'

And then Chris bent his head down to kiss me and it wasn't anything like it was with G. Because when Chris kissed me I knew I had his total, complete, undivided attention and he just made me feel that no other girl in the world was as special or beautiful as me. And it didn't matter that I wasn't blonde or hadn't got DD breasts. I knew I was just perfect the way I was. At least to him.

When the kiss finally ended he swept me up in his arms (sooo romantic) and we headed for the door. Hadn't realized that loads of people must have been listening to all that stuff I'd been saying to Chris until almost everyone around us burst into applause (including some of G's friends), which was quite embarrassing really. Although not as embarrassing as when Chris's friend Gary said that he'd found the on-stage snogging scene 'very, very exciting too' and when was I going to wear the nurse's uniform again?

Also heard comments such as, 'At long last' and 'Thank Christ, finally'. It seems that loads of people must have known that Chris fancied me for ages yet he never gave me even the slightest clue until Stephanie's party. Must speak to him about how stupid he's been one day soon.

Stephanie rang not long after Liz. She asked if Chris and I had used the WAP camera phone last night and if so demanded I send her the photos.

Confessed to Stephanie that Chris and I didn't actually have sex last night despite having the house to ourselves but made her promise not to tell Liz as I intend to torment her for a bit longer by supposedly withholding information.

In fact we had just spent the whole time kissing and talking and laughing and kissing some more. Well, OK, maybe a bit more than that but it's nice just to take time getting to know Chris as a boyfriend without the awful seven dates pressure I had with G.

Can't imagine what I ever saw in G to be honest. He was just a girlish crush really. Now that I am mature and sorted I expect that Chris and I will have an absolutely fantastic relationship based on perfect mutual trust.

SUNDAY DECEMBER 31ST

Which was why I wasn't bothered when Shelly rang today to say she was happy that Chris and I were an item and did I know she and G had got back together again? Feeling magnanimous, I told her I was happy for her too. Was also not at all concerned when she told me she'd seen Linda outside Chris's today and she was sure that they had just been exchanging a friendly goodbye kiss, which was probably why Chris hadn't bothered to mention it to me when he phoned.

Decided not to ask Chris about it. After all, a relationship based on perfect mutual trust doesn't need to discuss stuff like that, does it? Besides Shelly has said she'll keep an eye on things for me. Who'd have ever thought that Shelly and I would become friends?

Chris came over to my place to celebrate the New Year. Dad told Chris that he was pleased Chris and I were going out but also surprised, as last time they'd met he'd got the impression Chris swung the other way. Ha ha.

Mum told us that she hoped we weren't up to anything as one pregnant teenager in the family had been quite enough and she would go spare if we gave the neighbours anything more to talk about next year. She's got a nerve! Mum and Dad got quite pissed and had a fight as usual. Was so pleased they seemed to be back to their normal selves and that they had at last stopped their recent insufferable, 'it's-up-to-you-dear', 'no-no-it's-what-you-want-to-do-that-matters-love' phase.

Can't see Chris and me arguing ever about anything though.

MONDaY JaNUaRY 1 ST

Have just looked over my New Year resolutions of last year. Difficult to believe how totally naive and childish I was then. Have made new mature resolutions for this year:

My New Year Resolutions

1. Always to wear matching sexy underwear and never *ever* to put on grey knickers with worn elastic, and bras with saggy straps. Also the flannel Winnie-the-Pooh pyjamas that Aunt Kate bought me for my twelfth birthday have to go – no matter how warm and comfy they are in winter.

2. To exfoliate and de-fuzz my entire body each day so that every part of my skin is smooth, silky, and sensual to touch even though I am behind with my history project and I have to study for my

Higher prelims, which start at the beginning of January and on which my entire future academic success depends. Absolutely no excuses.

3. Never to kiss with morning breath or after onion, garlic or curry dishes. Even if it means I have to give up all the foods I really like and exist on tasteless nursery pap for the rest of my life.

4. Never to nag Chris about anything but to offer him loving support in all important areas of his life by giving him valuable advice on, for example, changing the really awful music he likes to listen to, getting rid of that totally sad jumper he always wears, and improving his taste in movies.

5. Never to tell Chris in an obvious crass way if he upsets me but instead to trust him to work out how I'm thinking and feeling for himself and to rely on him to intuitively know how to sort it out.

Just know this is going to be the most perfectly happy year of my whole life.